Mask

A Four Regions Story

Andrea Fink

Cover design and illustration by Jeff Brown Graphics

Published by

ANDREA FINK BOOKS

Dad,
I learned something.

Chapter One

She blinked up at the sky as she came to. Her head was spinning. She slowly began to make out shapes around her. The deep blue sky had streaks of thin, wispy clouds running through it. Far away, she could see a line of treetops to her left that abruptly gave way to the wide clearing in which she was lying. Soft stems radiated from multiple spots, pressing into her back and legs. She turned her head further; her long blonde hair was tangled in the tips of ferns.

"Don't stir yet," a man's voice said from her right. "It will take some time to adjust. Just relax." His voice was muffled and echoed within her own head.

She ignored the advice and tried to sit up, regretting it immediately. The entire earth shifted below her, tilting to the right. She fell back into the sea of ferns. Questions spun through her head—Where was she? How did they get here? Was anyone around to cry out to for help? Her mouth was dry as she began to speak, "What did you do to me?" It came out nearly a whisper.

There was a long pause before she felt his hand on her arm. The cold from his fingers spread through her arm quickly. Normally, the sensation would have given her chills, but in this instance it relaxed her tension. The stranger's touch was terrifying but steadying as it gave her a stable point of reference in this new place. Her senses began to clear. Birds chirped from far away in the bank of trees; no familiar calls, but she sensed they were peaceful sounds.

Despite his sudden speaking, the peaceful calm remained when he began, "I apologize for not asking your permission—I knew you would not believe what I had to tell you until we were here. My attempts to explain before were not successful, so I did what had to be done. I brought you here by a sort of portal—a tear in the world. I opened it to get to you and to bring you here. The journey can make many feel unsteady. You should be feeling well enough to get up soon and we can continue on. It would be beneficial to have context as I explain why you are so desperately needed."

As she continued to lay on the bed of ferns, her memory of the moments before her unconsciousness began to come back to her. She remembered the knock on her door; it was strong and abrupt. This lean, sharply-dressed man carrying an unconscious woman in his arms pushed by Emily to enter. The woman looked eerily familiar, but at the same time Emily did not recall ever meeting her. Emily felt unsafe around this stranger and concerned for the woman he carried. She had helped put the woman in her own bed while keeping the stranger in her sights in case he tried anything. Emily hadn't been drinking or eating anything, so he likely did not drug her in order to bring her to this place. He had told her that it was her sister. That was all she could recall. Again, her mind was flooded with questions. "I don't have a sister," is all she could manage to say.

"You do. She has lived here her whole life with your father. She is my dearest companion and -"

"I have no sister," She cut in. "I have no father. You have the wrong person. I'm going home. Please point me in the right direction." She again tried to get up but attempted it too quickly.

When she made it to her feet, she had to settle back down to the ground. She could see more now—the field of ferns reached for at least a hundred meters in every direction. To the left they continued into the wall of trees, which was as thick as if it were old-growth. To the right they reached until she could no longer see beyond them through a thick wall of fog. This field seemed to be a clearing between two walls. Before her was only the grass of ferns, so thick and lush she could only see green. Perhaps there was something else beyond the horizon, but for now all she knew was that there were ferns. She turned around to see a mountain range in the near distance behind her, while a dirt road crossed the field a few dozen meters away.

When she turned back around, he was standing in front of her with his hand stretched out. His blue coat sleeve was powdered with spores from the ferns. She took his hand and tried to use it to pull herself up, but instead he hoisted her up with ease. As she found her footing, she looked up into his face. His eyes were narrow but so dark she could not tell his iris from his pupil. His messy, dark hair was dusted with more spores. As he prepared to speak, his thin lips parted, letting out a deep sigh, "I suppose you're right. My apologies. Let me help you back to town so we can get this all sorted out. My name is Will."

She had no reason to trust him, but if he were going to harm her, she assumed he would have done so by now. She brushed off her sundress, which was also covered in debris from the ground. She felt scrapes up and down her arms. "I'm Emily," she said rather abruptly, "just show me the way home."

Emily stepped over and through clusters of ground cover which scratched at her calves, making her way slowly to the road she had seen before. She fell a handful of times—there was no set trail to go by. Will tried to help her up once or twice, but she shook him off each time—his cold hands no longer comforting, they just reminded her how dangerous this situation was. She hoped someone would drive by and offer them a ride so she

3

wouldn't have to be alone with him. As she reached the road, she found Will had already beaten her there, despite him following close behind her nearly the entire way.

He held his hand out to help her over the last bit and up onto the road, but she refused, instead choosing to clamber up rather clumsily. She again had to brush herself off, removing the fern bits, spores, and now dirt from her dress. The stains would not come out easily. She looked back toward Will to see his entire suit was spotless and his hair was neat, clean, and styled back. She thought to ask how but preferred to keep their conversation to a minimum. She just crossed her arms to point in both directions, as if to ask where they were headed.

He pointed to her left, into the fog that had not lifted since she had regained consciousness. She pivoted in that direction and began walking quickly. The sooner this adventure was over, the better. She had no idea where she was, so she already assumed it was going to be a long journey. The nearest forest to her city was at least twenty miles away, and this did not even look like that one. The mountain looked nothing like the mountains she could see from home, the trees did not look native to her area, not even the birds sounded familiar.

The flats on her feet began to dig into the backs of her heels. The soles of her feet became sore. Despite this, the wall of fog hardly seemed closer than it had been when they began walking. She turned around—still no cars to pick them up.

As she got closer to the wall of fog, it became cooler and cooler. She no longer felt comfortable in just her sundress. She wished she had a sweater with her—then she would have not only warmth but also pockets; her pockets would have her phone so she could call someone or even have a map to show her where to go so she wouldn't have to rely on this stranger. Just as she shivered, a coat went over her arms. She turned her head to see Will straighten the shoulder of his own coat over her shoulder and step back to his respectable following distance.

4

They came to the wall of fog and Emily stopped. It looked as if it were a storm churning behind a wall of glass. She reached out to touch it with just one finger. It was ice cold. As she withdrew her hand, a tuft of fog chased it, swirling and disappearing into the air around her. She looked to her side to find Will right there. He looked at her and nodded solemnly, closing his eyes as he did so. He then stepped into the fog, disappearing. The only trace of him was the fog that escaped the wall as he went in.

Emily turned around to look at the wall of trees in the far distance. She was tempted to walk toward them, away from this stranger and the abyss in her path, but the forest looked just as threatening. She took a deep breath and turned back to the fog. She saw an arm sticking out. The sleeve was rolled up and she noticed the definition in the muscles. The hand was held up, just as it had been when Will was offering to help her up onto the road. Emily took it and he pulled her in. The initial, painfully icy feeling lasted only a few seconds, but she continued to be unable to see for at least fifty steps. She wasn't sure if she should breathe in the vapor but knew she could not hold her breath the whole time. Will's hand pulled her along—and that was the only part of him she could see. She would not have been able to walk forward if it were not for him tugging at her. The sea of white slowly got darker—first in shades of gray, then a pitch black.

As the fog finally gave way, Emily saw Will against the backdrop of an old colonial town at night. The only light came from lamps in windows and hanging from doorways. It was quaint—like the setting of a movie about the American Revolution, but with an air of coziness. She hadn't seen any of the lights or heard any of the noises just moments before, but now she was standing just feet away from a building from which she could hear loud, live music and even louder shouting. She could smell coal burning, but not in crisp, cool air like she did at home. Instead, there was a humid evening coolness that foretold an impending storm.

Will turned toward Emily and readjusted her hand in his so he was holding just the fingertips. He looked into her eyes and she knew he was about to tell her something she wasn't going to want to hear, "I'm sorry to trick you into this, but I will do anything to save my fiancée's life. You are about to realize how much I am asking of you and it will not be fair to you. If you don't do as I say, however, you will be in even more danger than you are right now." His eyes shifted toward the door of the building, which was opening and letting out more of the clamor from inside. Someone was leaving.

While he was distracted, Emily snatched her hand away from his grip. She turned, determined to make a run for it when, without looking, his hand darted to her and grabbed her securely, but not forcefully, by the wrist. He looked back at her with even more concern in his eyes, almost pleading, but his voice was stern, "Your name is Daughter of Champion, but insist they call you Highness unless I indicate otherwise. There is no turning back now. You have to trust me and stay calm." He pulled her to the door.

Emily was startled by what she saw when she went inside. She tried to focus on the decor first. The brick walls were mostly free of decoration and painted white. There were metal tables and chairs toward the center of the room while the outer walls had booths made of stone. The floor, too, was made of stone. It was cold and unwelcoming at best, but the room was still filled with individuals. The sound of metal scraping against stone was frequent as patrons were constantly getting up, pushing their chairs out, and moving about. The patrons were hard to ignore, and not just because of the overwhelming noise they created with their conversations, arguments, and clumsy motions.

Emily's mind had trouble wrapping around what she was seeing. It was as if a circus sideshow act had been revived and had come to this town. At first glance, she saw whole groups of men who were uncommonly tall and slender. At one long table she saw more little people than she had ever seen in her life, not to mention more scattered about the room with other groups. As she continued to look more closely, things got even stranger. Not only were there people with eerily pale skin and white hair, but hues of skin and hair she did not think possible—purples, grays, and oranges. There were people covered with hair, people with scales, people with horns. One such person noticed them walk in, even amongst all of the commotion. He slammed down his drink, stood from his table, and walked toward them.

Emily got a better look at this—should she call it a person? He stood at least seven feet tall, broad-shouldered and muscular. His skin was gray and his black hair covered not only his head and chin, but also his legs where they protruded from pants that were made far too short for his height. Below his short, thick leg hair she was surprised to find hooves instead of shoes. She tried to imagine him walking on tiptoes or binding his feet to fit into the hooves. No matter how much she tried, she could not imagine a way to fit regular feet inside costumed hooves of that size. His horns came out of his forehead above his eyes and curved around the outside of his head, almost like a crown. He looked at Emily with the same curious fascination she must have been giving to him, though his was given with slightly less revulsion.

He stopped in front of her where she stood in the doorway and his deep voice boomed, "Highness, with all due respect, why are you wearing such ridiculous clothing? What would possess you to show that much skin?" The tables within earshot turned to look, as well.

Emily looked down at her sundress, then back at the patrons of this establishment. She was clearly inappropriately dressed. Although this place seemed very casual, everyone was dressed in fashions reminiscent of days long ago, when even the working-class men would wear a neck scarf to work and women wore only full-length dresses with coats. Her bare calves felt very out of place. The chevron pattern of her sundress seemed out of date. "I…" she began, pulling Will's coat tighter across her chest.

She didn't notice that Will had entered the door and stood beside her. "You would not believe us if we told you." His voice sounded relaxed and cunning—a tone Emily had not heard from him before. Will laughed and patted the monster on the arm with his right hand, and the horned man did the same. "Good to see you, Brawn."

"And you, your Lordship," Brawn's focus was on Will now, though he glanced over occasionally to eye Emily's attire, "What brings you to our edge of the world? Nothing too political, I hope." He stepped back to examine Will's outfit, "You look in a state yourself. Where did you get these dressings? They look like they were made for one half your size." Brawn pulled at the collar of the fitted, button-up white shirt with his massive fingers.

Will chuckled again, his eyes nearly disappearing as his cheeks rose. He had told her there would be danger, but she could not tell by his attitude. "I assure you, they were appropriate for the time and place of our business, but now we must change." Without another word, he again patted Brawn's arm and walked off to what looked to be the bar.

"Aye," he slammed his hand against the stone bar and got the attention of a slender, pale woman with long, braided red hair and red eyes who was cleaning a mug, "Her Highness and I each require a room for the day, and may I please have the bags I left yesternight."

She handed him two bags from behind the bar and pulled out a large book and a quill, "Sign here."

Will signed "Will of Capital" on the first available line. He let his left hand linger on the page as he handed the quill to Emily.

As she approached the book, she noticed his finger was on the word "Capital" and he tapped it twice before moving away. Emily squared herself to write, blowing on the page lightly to dry the ink Will left before signing—a habit picked up from a lifetime of ink staining the side of her left hand as she wrote. She noticed the book was not made of paper, but rather bound parchment. She signed "Daughter of Champion of Capital" in cursive on the space under Will's name. It had been ages since she'd written anything but her own signature in cursive, it felt clumsy and unnatural—even stranger than writing someone else's name.

The barkeeper closed the book and placed it back behind the bar, exchanging it for two copper keys, "Nine and ten. Out by two hours after dark. No exceptions, even for her," she cocked her head toward Emily.

Chapter Two

They ascended a metal staircase in the back and came to the third floor where they stopped at rooms with metal doors and numbers nine and ten engraved on them. Will held one of the bags out to her, which seemed to be made of animal hide. She opened it to find deep purple cloth bundled up inside. Will also handed her the key with "10" engraved on it, "Go get dressed, take a moment to yourself. I will be in the next room ready for questions. Can I trust you to be on your own?"

Emily could only nod. She had been able to say one word since she arrived, and even that had been a struggle in her state of confusion. She wouldn't dare go back downstairs alone. She wasn't sure she'd be able to go back down even with company, but she knew she wouldn't have to until two hours after dark. But what time was it? How long did she have? She unlocked the room and the heavy door squeaked on the hinges. She locked it behind her. Inside was a simple bed and a metal dresser—that was it. Emily threw herself and the bag onto the bed, upon which was a pelt blanket. Emily curled up on her side and ran her fingers through the animal's soft fur. She lay there for what seemed like both an instant and an eternity, grounding herself in the calm and quiet of the unfamiliar room.

There was no sideshow. This was no convention. This was no film set. She was in a real place with real monsters and a charming stranger whom she had just met told her she was in real danger. She weighed her options. She could run away, back to the ferns, and try to find her way on her own. She would have to go through the bar, though. Brawn might see her—*anyone* might see her—and mistake her for this other person again. She would have no idea where to go, how to find this...portal, was it? How would it even work? Her other option would be to march into the next room and ask these questions. She slid her fingers deep into the blanket and sighed, giving in to her curiosity.

Emily dumped the bag out to find the purple cloth was actually a full-length dress. Under it was a sort of coat with long sleeves and a skirt she assumed would go under the dress. She had to lay the entire ensemble out on the bed a few times to figure out how it went—a cloth puzzle. There were stiff parts and flexible parts, but a series of buttons helped her figure out what needed to attach where. That was not even the hardest part—navigating her way through the parachute's worth of fabric took physical exertion for which Emily was not prepared. Buttons and bows made her fingers sore from the fine motor work. Thankfully, she wore a strapless bra that day under her sundress, so she would not have too many problems hiding her undergarments.

Once the dress was on, she noted the extra volume in the form of ruffles in the back of the skirt and the cinching around the elbow of the coat. The dress itself needed to be tightened in the back, but she could not manage without help. She did the best she could and tucked the strings into the shoulder so she could reach them later, covering it all up with the coat that she buttoned to a type of breastplate. Without a mirror to look in, she felt unsure of whether she had done it up right, but her curiosity was overpowering her vanity. She left the room and locked the door behind her—she had nothing that needed to be kept safe, but it was habit. She tucked the key into her sleeve, as she doubted this dress would have pockets.

Will's door was open. He was seated on the bed, not having changed out of his out-of-place suit, watching the doorway. His eyes became more alert when she came into view, "You look exquisite. The dress suits you," he stood and stammered a bit, "I mean, it fits. I'm glad. I was worried you might not be the same size as your sister." He closed the door behind her and locked it. Emily felt she had just placed herself in a precarious situation until Will handed her the key. Will's fingers just brushed Emily's palm and, despite the warmth of the room, his fingers were still colder than ice.

His eyes were welcoming and soft, understanding her confusion. Emily had no idea where to begin. She waited for his explanation. They stood in silence, each waiting for the other to speak.

They locked eyes for an uncomfortable amount of time. Noticing this, she turned to scan the room. It also had just a bed and a dresser. No fireplace, no mirror, no artwork. Just a plain, basic room for sleeping—or whatever else might happen in a bed. Not facing him made it easier to ask questions.

She was about to speak when Will, also no longer hypnotized by the awkward eye contact, spoke, "Daughter of Champion is my fiancée. She is your sister; identical by the looks of it. They assume you are her because you are so similar—all but your hair and markings."

Emily remembered the woman who was brought into her apartment. She had dark brown hair and tattoos down her arm like tiger stripes. Other than that, Emily supposed they looked alike, but her face had always seemed generic—a good quarter of people of Scandinavian descent could be confused as

12

relatives. She hadn't thought to take out a mirror and compare their features—she had more pressing concerns at the time.

"What kind of name is Daughter of Champion?" Emily asked after her train of thought was broken by a crash from downstairs.

"She hasn't had her trial yet. Your name is chosen by a tribunal after your first major challenge in life. Sometimes they happen organically and when something life-defining occurs. If it doesn't happen by your twentieth year, the tribunal puts you in a battle or survival situation. Whatever skill or character trait you display most prominently becomes your name. Your sister, like you, has nineteen years. Her trial was in the process of being arranged when she fell ill. She brought situations to the tribunal multiple times, when she did political work for your father, but it is not traditional for females to have names of the mind—and her talents are mostly academic and diplomatic. Females go by 'Daughter of' the father and males by 'Son of' the father, or their mother if they are fatherless."

"How did her dad get the name Champion?" Emily asked, ensuring to call him *her* dad and not *our* dad. She hadn't yet bought into the idea of having a sister or a father.

"When the last ruler was killed, he had no named heirs. He had a young daughter who was still years away from her trial, but none who qualified to rule. So a Grand Trial was held—any named individual was eligible to fight to the death to claim the throne. Your father, known as Dagger back then, was a low-level thief who lurked in the shadows around Capital. He had nothing to lose and entered himself into the competition. When all of his opponents either surrendered or were killed, he became Champion—a name only conferred on those who claim the throne by battle."

"Will seems like a normal enough name, though," she turned to him, he smirked.

"Not William like in your world," he was amused enough by the comment to give a small chuckle, "*Will* as in determination. I had a trial that seemed impossible, but never stopped. It took weeks before I overcame it."

Another pause ensued as Will waited for another question to guide the conversation. He sat down at the foot of the bed. Emily went to the window to look outside. Individuals were hurrying this way and that on the streets below. Many wore dark cloaks with hoods, large hats, and other outerwear that suggested it was going to rain or that they didn't want to be seen. On the horizon, day was beginning to break. "What about them? What are they?"

Will smiled as if he knew a great secret but wanted the other party to guess, "I would assume they still tell the stories to children where you are from—the dark creatures that trick and lure and stalk and kill humans."

Emily asked about the first to come to mind, "So, vampires?"

Will nodded, "Yes, but none here tonight. You would have caused quite the commotion coming in with your human blood. They typically congregate separately."

"Dwarves? Not someone with the medical condition but, like, mining dwarves with beards?"

"Yes, in a way. They are not just miners—they are a diverse group, but many are involved in trade, especially in metals and jewels. Most reside in the mountains, of course, but many journey here to the edge of this region for trade and recreation. The beard is not common to all dwarves, though."

Emily wasn't sure yet if she'd believed it, but she racked her brain for all of the mythological creatures she could think of, "Elves?"

"Yes."

"Dragons?"

"In the mountains."

"Mermaids?"

14

"Here they go by the name of siren, but yes, only in the Seas."

"Kraken?"

"There is just one, and he is ancient now."

"Witches?"

"Yes and no. The use of magic is widespread, but none would call themselves simply a 'witch' or 'wizard.' Their powers come from their distinct race and they would identify themselves by that instead."

"Who gets to use magic, then?"

"Elves, fairies, and demons are typically the most powerful, but almost everyone here is able to access power to some degree."

"Can humans do magic?" Emily had always toyed with the idea of being able to do magic—a feeling of power she never had as a kid. She read fantasy books about witches and wizards defeating dark powers, but left those stories behind when she grew up.

"No, but there are no true humans in this region. There are legends of humans in other regions, but none here. Some can trace part of their lineage back to a human, but pure human blood no longer exists."

Emily had been scanning the streets during the conversation, but spun to face Will, "You? Aren't you human?"

Will closed his eyes and shook his head, grinning slightly, "Demon. No human blood that I know of or that anyone can sense." He opened his eyes, but he still looked down at the floor. He was waiting for something.

Emily realized what it was, "So I am the only human?"

Will kept his body hunched over and his head low, but finally looked up at her. Emily realized his eyes were not just dark like they were when she first met him, but they had no whites at all. His eyebrows showed hesitance of what he was about to say— sympathy mixed with pity, "No. Not completely."

Emily was done asking questions. She didn't like the game they were playing anymore. She wanted more than what Will was telling her. She crossed her arms and gave Will a look as if to say "and…?"

"You're part demon, too. You never could have known when you lived where you did because you have no markings, your mother was completely human, and you had no access to your powers in a world void of magic. You are half demon, though. Since you looked human, you were the one who was sent to live with your mother. It was safer for you."

Emily enjoyed the talk of mythical creatures walking among her, even the revelation that her current companion was not what she had assumed, but this last disclosure was a step too far to be believed, even in her exhausted and confused state. The only thing she could think to say was "Prove it."

"Prove what?"

"Any of it!" Her voice raised and she was beginning to sound hysterical. Whatever this was, she wanted no part of it. "Just prove it!"

Will sat for a moment, considering what to do. He sighed as he got up off of the bed and sat down on the floor in front of Emily. He held up his left hand toward her and said, "Sit."

Emily took his hand for support and sat, somewhat awkwardly in the skirt, with a look of extreme skepticism on her face. He held her right hand in his left and placed his right hand on her shoulder. He closed his eyes in deep concentration, taking deep breaths and mumbling to himself. He gently ran his hand down her right sleeve, holding her hand in both of his as he finished. The action made Emily's face soften and she looked up to meet his eyes as he opened them. The darkness of them should have been terrifying, but they were fascinating to her— no definition between the iris and pupil, no whites at all, just black. Will brought out a knife and, before Emily could pull away, he cut the sleeve of the coat up to the elbow. On Emily's skin was tattooed the same stripes that were on Daughter of Champion's arm. Her left hand felt the markings—it was her skin, nothing had been applied to it, but it looked completely changed. It didn't even look quite like a tattoo—the blackness of it was too dark to come from a pigment and it wasn't raised or red.

"Perhaps it would be more convincing if you tried something yourself?" Will suggested, sensing Emily was trying to figure out a simple explanation for what just happened.

"Perhaps," she agreed in a soft whisper.

"Alright, then. Let us get you dressed," Will pulled Emily to her feet, helped her remove the coat, and untucked the strings from where she had placed them on her shoulder. Emily felt the ends fall onto the fabric of her dress skirt. Will stood shoulder-to-shoulder with Emily and held out his hands in front of him, as if he were holding a horse's reins. He nodded to Emily, indicating to do the same. She held her hands out, too. "Feel the strings in your hand." He rubbed his thumb against his forefinger where a string might fall if he were holding them. Emily did the same. She hadn't completely bought in but was going to at least try it the way he told her. "Now pull."

She pulled abruptly at the imaginary string and, as she did so, the dress tightened around her chest and middle. She was forced to straighten her back in order to breathe comfortably. The ends of the strings bounced and fell further down on her legs.

"Now, tie it," Will suggested, leaving Emily's side to watch her better.

Emily flailed her hands around haphazardly, pantomiming tying a bow. She could no longer feel the ends of the string on her back.

Will walked around to see her work, "Do you not know how to tie a proper knot? You have secured it well, but I worry about how you will take this off to sleep." He began picking at the large knot she created. It took him a minute or two to successfully solve the puzzle, "Try again, but in earnest."

She took the imaginary strings in her hand. It was hard to tie a bow without physical feedback or looking—she was like a child trying to tie her shoes again, needing to analyze every step in the process. When she finished, she felt secure in the dress. Her hands were sore as if she had been gripping the string for hours, but she had just done a trick fairly successfully. It was no teleportation, but she had a sense of accomplishment in performing it.

"It will be tiring at first while you build up your endurance," Will commented when he saw Emily massaging her hands, "but it will become simpler and more natural."

"Getting dressed or magic in general?"

"Both, I suppose. I leave the next part up to you—would you like to go downstairs to eat or eat in your room? The kitchen closes at sunup, but I can probably convince them to make something special." Will walked toward the door, patted his pocket, and reached out to Emily for the key.

"I'll eat in my room," Emily slipped the key from her uncut sleeve. The fabric dangled from her right arm as she did, "I have a lot to think about right now, and I am not sure if I could muster sitting down there with all of...them." She walked over to Will and handed him the key. She looked down at her marked arm.

"They'll all be gone by now. Not many of them can tolerate the sunlight well and protection magic is difficult when one has been at the drink." He reached out for the key and again took her hand. It felt more comfortable to Emily now, letting his cold hands touch hers. He folded the ripped cloth back over her arm and ran his hand down it. The sleeve was repaired instantly with no indication it had ever been in such bad shape. She remembered back to the field when his suit stayed immaculate despite trudging through thick undergrowth. When he withdrew his hand, the key was gone. He opened the door and signaled for her to go through with a sweeping arm, "but I can understand if you want some privacy at the moment, Highness."

The stark realization that she had to pretend to be someone else hit her. She had to be someone who was comfortable here. Someone who could use magic for more than just getting dressed. Someone who was already engaged to this man who cared so much about her that he would kidnap someone to save her. It didn't feel as unfair now, though. She could learn about this world, about how to use magic, and possibly get to meet her dad if she was really who Will thought she was. None of that would matter when she got home, but it would be an experience.

Emily was still standing in front of the open door while Will continued to hold it, gesturing. She collected herself and stood up a little straighter. Daughter of Champion was royalty, after all, and she would have to act the part. Her dress gently brushed the stone floor—it was a perfect fit now that it was on properly. She always enjoyed the confidence that came with a new outfit and, although she couldn't see herself wearing it in a mirror, she knew she wore it well. She felt more powerful, beautiful, and confident in this moment than she had in a long time. She unlocked the door to her room and the change of scenery brought the reality of it all crashing down on her. She pushed the door closed behind her, forgetting to lock it.

Emily fell to the bed crying—this confidence only came from pretending to be someone else. Again, she ran her fingers through the furs on the bed and blocked out all thoughts besides the feel of the fur on her fingers. It was safe, it was comfortable, and nobody expected anything of her while she was alone in this room. She realized how tired she was and allowed herself to fall asleep with the sun beaming in through her window.

When she opened her eyes, she saw an orange glow through the slats of the window—someone had come in and shut them. She saw small particles floating through the concentrated beams of light. She moved her hand over the furs and more dust was swept up into the air, creating a beautiful trail through the light. There was a burnt smell lingering in the room, like someone had lit and extinguished a candle. It hadn't been a dream—she was still in this small, undecorated, cold room, and now the dark creatures would be back when the sun went back down, and she would have to go out among them.

Will knocked, then let himself in. He was carrying a tray with food. "I came to give it to you earlier, but you'd fallen asleep. I kept it warm for you." He set the tray on the bed next to where she was laying, then stood by the dresser, leaning his hip on it with his arms crossed.

Emily sat up and stretched—sleeping in such a constricting dress did not do much for comfortable sleep. She looked down at the food: a ceramic plate with meat and potatoes. Not her typical fare, but she was hungry enough to eat anything. She shifted herself to the foot of the bed and balanced the tray on her lap as she ate.

"In the future, we will need some sort of code," Will noted, "Your sister and I had one to make sure nobody was impersonating me to get to her."

"I guess it didn't work, then, if someone was able to make her unconscious," Emily said with a half-full mouth. She realized she hadn't eaten since the morning she was taken from her apartment—she had been making lunch when she was interrupted by Will carrying her supposed sister. She was not sure how much time had passed since then, but it had to be at least a full twenty-four hours.

Will, who had been looking at the ground so as not to stare at someone who was eating, looked up, "You might be right. I hadn't considered that. It will need to be a new code, then. It used to be a special way I grabbed her hand when we met. Maybe someone picked up on that."

Emily, feeling a little more comfortable now that she had accepted the basic premise of her being here and had remedied her empty stomach, made a suggestion, "A special kiss, then?" She felt bold, suggesting a kiss from another woman's fiancé, but if it was to be a believable greeting, they would have to show affection.

Will chuckled slightly, "Not our typical manner, but I suppose it would be appropriate." He walked across the room to where Emily was sitting. He leaned down and his hands rested on the bed on either side of her hips, reaching over the balancing tray. Emily's eyes widened—she had just stuffed another potato into her mouth and was in the process of chewing it, but she paused when she realized what was happening. His head went to her right and he whispered in her ear, "Remember how this feels." His breath was cool, but not cold. Goosebumps covered her arms as he gently kissed her right cheek, directly on her cheekbone.

As he pulled away, she exhaled. It was innocent, yet incredibly sensual at the same time. She shook her head to clear it and finished the bite of food that was in her mouth, "I think that will work, if you think my sister would be alright with it."

"She has no choice," he shrugged, "we need people to believe you are her and do so quickly. Making our relationship clear will reinforce the performance."

Emily wiped her mouth and set the tray to her side. "How am I supposed to pretend to be her if I've never met her? I don't know anything about her, not to mention her mannerisms and the little things people might pick up on. How many people know she is sick? What if someone gives me up?"

"Let me assure you, not many people know at all. It is just me and the person who found her, and he is a close friend. Your father doesn't even know. Her lady-in-waiting doesn't know, and they are as close as two can be. They will be the hardest to convince, but not many others know her on a deep level. It is not them I worry about, but it is the people who dislike her we will need to satisfy. If we can find anyone who is surprised by your sister's presence, that will be a good start."

"Why didn't you tell her dad? Shouldn't he be the one coming to get his supposed 'other daughter?'"

"Do not think I did not want to tell him. He is away on regional business. I do not have the authority to ask where he has gone or for how long. The only way I could have gotten that information was by telling his advisors about the illness, but I do not trust them. Now, if he found out that I brought you here, he would be furious. He is known for his temper."

Processing this, Emily realized there was more to unpack. "Wait, are you saying I get to meet a man you claim is my father and not tell him who I am just to save your skin?"

"You are not here to have a relationship with your father. You are here to save your sister. That is all."

"And when I save her, what then? She comes back and I go home, no dad, no sister, just me on my own again?"

"Yes," Will hissed, his tone turned harsh. Any warm feelings Emily had gotten from the kiss were gone. This wasn't a friendship, this wasn't him caring about her; it was her being there for a mission and getting cast away when it was over.

"And if I decide I want to stay?" Emily became defiant and loud, "What then? Will you force me to go back home? Just use me and get rid of me? Will I not even get to tell my dad I'm alive? Does he even know I exist?" She realized that she had stood up during her questioning and her face was hot.

Will kept a quiet tone, but Emily could tell he was getting impatient, "You will not meet your father as yourself. He is not to know you are here. You are forbidden from ever stepping foot here because you are a threat to your sister. She is older, but if you are named before she is, she loses her place. In order to keep the precarious inheritances tidy, the younger sibling is often disposed of, but your father sent you away with your mother so you could live. Your sole reason for being here is to save my fiancée. That is it. You two cannot exist in the same place, so when she comes back you will leave."

Emily began to feel the weight of how unfair the situation was. If it was all true, she was expected to use herself as bait to find the person who tried to kill her sister, interact with her own estranged father while pretending to be someone else, learn to use powers that she could never use again, and be cast aside the moment it was all over. She did not like this place, but she was not all too fond of home, either. Something snapped, making her realize how pathetic she had been behaving. "No," she said sternly, "I'm not going to do it." She turned away toward the door, but Will grabbed her wrist firmly. His normally cold touch was hot—burning hot. She looked down at where he was grabbing her and saw fire surrounding his hand and her wrist.

He pulled her toward him and brought his face close to hers, "I have no patience for this. I do not know how much time your sister has before whatever has befallen her kills her," He spoke sternly and quietly as if disciplining a small child, "You are going to do this because she is your sister. You are going to do this to save your father's legacy. You are going to do this because if you do not, you will be stranded in a strange place with no resources and no way home, surrounded by creatures of the dark. You are in a very unfortunate place and you do not have any leverage in this negotiation." He threw her hand down.

Emily looked at her wrist—there was a slight burn mark in the shape of his fingers and thumb all the way around. She looked at him, disbelieving. When he saw her face, he lowered his head apologetically, "I forgot myself. I am frustrated and desperate. I feel alone in this and cannot conceive a way in which I can help her myself. She is the smart one in our partnership. She is the one who plans and figures and reasons. I am the one who supports. I need her."

"Well, you don't have her." Emily kept her volume low, but her tone was harsh, "As much as I can pretend to be her, I will never be her. I don't figure or reason or plan. I have strong emotions and I am not afraid to express them. I am almost constantly either anxious or distracted. I have terrible ideas and go with them. I am not the person who is going to save her. You are going to need to step up and have a plan. I am not going into this blind. If I help, I am going to get something out of it, including, but not limited to, a promise that I can go home when I choose, even if it is before we fix things. I'm not going to act selflessly for someone I've never met and didn't even know existed until yesterday," She grabbed his chin firmly and forced him to look her in the eye, "And you will not speak to me like I am a child. I am a grown-ass woman who is doing you a favor and I will not be taking shit from you. Do I make myself clear?"

Will smiled, but his chin was still firmly in Emily's hand, so his cheeks were pushed up comically. Emily noticed why he was amused—her hand was on fire. She didn't feel it burning, but a small flame encased her hand as if it was covered in a thin layer of lighter fluid. She let go quickly and shook her hand to extinguish the flame. She examined her hand and it showed no signs of having been on fire just moments before. She turned to Will, "Magic?"

He nodded, "You have a lot to learn. I'd be willing to teach you more on the way to Capital, if you'd do me the honor of joining me on my journey." He bowed gracefully before adding, "Your Highness."

As upset as Emily was, she couldn't help but be intrigued by the prospect of learning magic. Will also hadn't given her the alternative of leaving. She composed herself, pulled her sleeve down over the burn on her wrist, and packed her belongings away inside the bag Will had given her. She walked out the door, down the stairs, and outside without even glancing at the patrons. A man was standing outside of a metal-framed carriage with no horses, bowing toward Emily. This must be her ride.

Chapter Three

Emily could feel every cobblestone under the carriage wheels. It wasn't an uncomfortable ride, in fact, the suspension was astounding for the simple design, but she was very aware of everything around her. She felt the ruching on the back of her dress, uncomfortable under her legs. The burn on her wrist felt tight with a stinging sensation. Her hands grazed the velvet upholstery on the bench; Will sat on a bench opposite, facing Emily. She did not look at him. Her focus was out the window. The stars had come out and they were brighter and more brilliant than any she had seen at home. She didn't recognize any of the constellations, but she did see a moon. It didn't look like *the* moon, but it was *a* moon. It was full and brilliant. The air felt heavy, but cool on her neck and forearms—the only parts this dress left exposed to the elements.

It had been at least six hours since the sun set, but she wasn't tired; she had slept all day. It was the start of summer at home—the days were long and the nights were only a few hours. Although she was still unsure of how she wanted to interact with Will, her curiosity got the better of her, "How does time work?"

she asked, still looking out the window. It sounded like such an existential question, but she assumed he knew what she really meant.

"Much like yours, but more consistent," Will was looking directly at her—she could feel his gaze, "There are no seasons—in this region nights are always 16 hours and days are always eight. It's better for our inhabitants that way, as most have low or no tolerance for sunlight. Passage of time is the same; we even use the same calendar, though we count our years from the date of independence from the human world."

Emily fell silent again. They had left the town at the edge of the region, which she came to find out was named simply "Edge." The area in between towns was bare. Emily couldn't see trees or farms, just empty land. It was dark, but she expected to see at least the outline of something along the side of the road. Maybe a light from a farmhouse or another carriage. The only light came from the towns they left and the towns they were approaching, though she could sense there was something out in the vast darkness. The drive was taking so long with only watching the darkness to pass the time. They passed through the towns of "Poison Lake" and "Midway" without problem, but Emily began to grow bored of the silence.

She looked at Will. He was still looking at her—had he not looked away this whole time? "How much longer?"

Will shrugged, "We will not be there until after the next nightfall. There are still hours to go."

"Teach me something," Emily said as she held out her hands, palm-up, toward him. She was not going to tolerate another period of silence, especially if there was still a long way to travel.

Will leaned forward and traced his fingertips along her palms, "Your appearance is very deceiving. You channel a lot of energy through you, more than your sister. I feel you can do great things with that power if you can control it." He pushed up her sleeve and revealed the burned skin, "Certain power is closely tied to emotion. For example, anger," he held Emily's hand while rubbing his thumb over the mark, "elicits heat and fire. Compassion and affection, on the other hand," he took his hand and held it over her wrist, "is linked with healing." A warmth and a tingling sensation radiated from Will's hand. When he removed it, the burn had gone, as well as the itching pain that accompanied it. He averted his eyes and his tone became sheepish, "Do not mention what I just did to anyone around here. The healing arts are frowned upon in the region."

Emily could sense Will's discomfort and wanted to change the subject. "You keep talking about this region, but what about the other regions?" Emily asked as she sat back on her bench. At one point along the journey she had been thinking about all of the mythical creatures she'd heard of in her life and placing where they might live, "The dwarves are in the mountains and mermaids in the seas—are there any others?"

"There are four regions that have government," Will sat back on his bench, matching Emily's posture, "the Mountains, the Seas, the Dark Region, and the Light Region. In the middle of the four is a sort of lawless juncture known as the Null. This is where I brought you first—it was less likely we would be found out since not many travel through there."

The next hours were a history lesson of the Regions. Emily learned about the creatures who felt the need to leave what was now the human world after waves of witch trials and executions left them feeling uneasy. For thousands of years, many magical beings had the ability to travel to another plane—a barren wasteland made up of rocks and seas—and would often go there to flee from immediate danger. Some individuals began creating shelters there as a safe haven for weary travelers. Around the early 1600s, some of the most powerful creatures of the time came together to create a whole world in this plane for magical creatures to inhabit safely. It took nearly 200 years and exhausted some powerful beings to the point of death, but the project continued in the hopes it would become home to all magic folk. As more and more creatures made it their permanent residence, the four regions were designated when it was realized that certain races could not live among each other. Each created its own government based on their own needs. After all magical creatures came to this new place in the late 1700s, it became law that none would venture back to the human world without permission from the leaders of their region and the portal was closed to all except those with part human blood. Those with human family were still allowed to visit, but if they used magic in the human world, they were to be put to death for risking exposing their secret. Once magical blood was essentially eliminated from the human world and magical creatures no longer had close relations in the human world, the portal was permanently closed.

"Obviously it wasn't permanent," Emily interrupted his monologue, "otherwise I wouldn't be here, or my sister for that matter."

"Your father was never one for rules," Will smiled. "He was fascinated by the human world. There had been no contact for nearly a hundred years, but he had studied humans extensively once he had access to the royal library. He was strong enough to create a new temporary portal and did so with the intention of observing and bringing back books and artifacts. He went to purchase books and a lovely young woman helped him. He returned to that store time and time again. She showed him books about modern history, and he told her tales of fantasy.

"He brought her back, hid her in the palace, and they were happily and secretly married for a few years before a vampire visiting the palace smelled the human blood. He revealed their secret, but by that time she was already pregnant. Rioters tried to break in to kill them both, but your father held them off long enough for her to give birth. They threatened to kill all four of you if she stayed, so for your safety they agreed to send her back with the child who was more likely to fit in in the human world. Your sister says he never loved again, but also never risked your mother's safety by going back for the both of you."

Memories of Emily's late mother floated across her mind. She worked in that bookshop for Emily's whole life—in fact, she bought it from the owner when Emily was just starting school. Emily did her homework on the floor behind the counter as her mother worked. Her mom used to tell stories of dark creatures far more than any other fairy tales—had they been based on her experience in this place? The antagonist was frequently a vampire; perhaps she held a grudge. She, too, had never fallen in love again. When Emily asked about her father, her mom would simply sigh and say, "All you need to know is that he loved us both," and kiss her on the forehead. She died from breast cancer when Emily was only 16, leaving her on her own. The sale of the bookstore covered hospital and funeral costs and kept Emily housed and fed until she finished high school—she was just scraping by when Will found her.

Day was starting to break over the horizon. The shades of the carriage were drawn, and Will retreated into a corner where the sunlight that snuck through the edges didn't touch him. He removed his coat and laid it over himself as he tried to fall asleep. Emily was tired and felt sleep would be the best way to pass the remaining hours. She removed her coat and looked at the markings on her right arm—a reminder that she was not here for herself—and the site of the burn beneath it. She stopped to stare at Will in admiration. He was so powerful, but he looked so peaceful in this moment. She knew he cared deeply for her sister, but he hardly spoke about her except in a tone of obligation.

Emily must have dozed off because she awoke to Will's soft lips on her cheek, just under the edge of her right eye. He whispered in her ear, "It's me. We've arrived."

Once again, his breath on her skin caused a rush of emotions—none of which she was proud of since they were elicited by someone who had little affection for her and who was engaged to somebody else, but she couldn't mentally overpower her craving for affection. She opened her eyes to see darkness once again outside of the carriage windows, but there were a row of lamps illuminating the face of the beautiful brick mansion in front of which they had stopped, "Is this the palace?"

"No," Will shook his head as he stepped out of the carriage door, "I've taken the liberty of taking you to my house for the evening—I have business to attend to and was hoping you would assist me." He held out his hand to help her from the carriage.

Emily felt clumsy stepping down in her half-asleep state in a dress that felt just too wide for the carriage door. Will's hand kept her steady; while she was shaking slightly, he was completely unmoving, like he was made of stone. He was looking up at her admiringly—a show put on for the staff that was welcoming him back, Emily realized. When she reached the ground, Will turned and placed Emily's hand in the bend of his elbow.

The house rose three stories in front of them, with a round turret on each side of the building's face. In the torchlight, the red brick glowed warmly. The windows were large on the first floor and grew smaller on each level, a handful of them glowing with firelight from inside.

Two men dressed in embellished coats and short pants with long socks opened the large french doors at the entrance as they approached. Will nodded at them both as they passed through the doors into a grand foyer. Emily was stunned by the elegance of it. The ceiling was two stories tall with double curved staircases leading to a second story. A large chandelier hung above them. The flickering of candles through dozens of colors of glass illuminated the walls—ambers, reds, and purples danced across the stone walls. Huge tapestries hung from the walls, images of romanticised vampires, demons, and other terrifying monsters attacking humans who were either shown as the enemy or the prey, depending on the context. She didn't have much time to admire every detail, as Will's hand was on top of hers on his arm and he pulled her along when she tried to stop and take it all in. He brought them directly to a door to the side of the right staircase, opened the door, and allowed her to enter first.

Inside was a cozy library with thick, leather-bound books on shelves that lined every wall. There were intricate statues on shelves and on the large desk in the middle of the room. The overall ambiance of the library felt strange, though, as there was not a single item or surface made of wood. In fact, Emily realized she hadn't seen wood at all since she walked away from the bank of trees—no wooden doors, furniture, floors, beams, or even carriages. It was all metal and stone. Emily opened a book that was on the stone slab desk—no paper, only parchment, just like at the pub. The book was titled *Advanced Travel*. The page it fell open to was a chapter on portals with cross-references and other notes in the margins.

Will dismissed the young man who was cleaning the library, asking for privacy for regional business, "But if you see Wit, it may be useful for him to join us." The young man nodded in a sort of bow and closed the door behind him as he left.

Will seemed to have anticipated Emily's realization, "Vampires are very politically powerful here. Wood and other such products have been illegal since the beginning of the region. They nearly outlawed all vegetation completely, but other races managed to secure root vegetables since the part that would be imported doesn't touch the sun. Anything that gets energy from the sun is toxic to them. Prepare to eat a lot of meat and to wear a lot of wool."

Emily was suddenly very aware of her underskirt. It was unbearably itchy against her thighs. She found a cushioned seat in the corner and sat down, tucking her knees up into one side and her feet into the other, draping her skirt over the front of the chair. The back of her calves met the back of her thighs and the feeling of her own skin was so much smoother than the provided dress. Will watched her the whole time—he was not as mystified by the library as she was, but she was something new in the room. Emily tried not to meet his eyes, but she could feel his gaze the whole time. Instead she alternated between toying with the fabric of her skirt and admiring the stone moulding at the ceiling. The silence became too much and, just as she was about to speak, the door opened.

In walked—no, walked is too clumsy to describe how he entered—in *glided* the most beautiful man Emily had ever seen. His hair was the lightest shade of blond it could be before being classified as white. It was slicked back with a little volume given to it in the front. It was convenient that it was styled that way, as it was kept out of his face, which was like that of an ancient Roman sculpture. He had a strong jawbone and well-defined cheekbones. He was tall and thin, but not gaunt. When he saw Emily, his face shifted from cordiality to surprise and then to disgust.

His eyes shot to Will. His voice was deep and soft, but concerned, "Will, tell me my eyes deceive me. Tell me that you did not go forward with your preposterous plan!"

"It was my only choice," Will loudly whispered through gritted teeth as he walked over quickly and closed the door behind the newcomer, "Wit, this is Emily."

Emily realized she was still staring—*gawking*, rather—at the stranger like a wide-eyed schoolgirl. Her breath seemed to have left her along with her senses. Emily fumbled to get her dress out of her way as she tried to get out of the chair to introduce herself. It was the most clumsy she'd ever felt, though she had

33

never been particularly graceful. When she finally got to her feet, she lunged toward Wit with her hand outstretched, going in to shake his hand. She aborted that course of action quickly when she saw him recoiling. Still, she made her way toward the newcomer.

The disgust hadn't left Wit's expression, as he bluntly stated, "You reek."

Emily stopped in her tracks, "Excuse me?" She was at least a meter or two away from him. Her tone was not indignant, but rather unbelieving. She was so confident he was feeling the same connection that his words took her aback.

A look of realization came across Will's face, though Emily was so entranced by Wit that she barely noticed, "I am so sorry, Wit." Will raced to the shuttered window and opened it wide, letting the cool night air in, "She arrived yesterday. She has not had time to bathe. I had her change her clothes, but..."

"Her hair," Wit cut in, with a tone both intrigued and disgusted, "It has been so long since I've smelled such pure human scent. But fruit, too. A nauseating stench of fruit is carried with it."

Emily had showered the night before she left. She used tropical, fruity shampoo—could he really smell it like some sort of scent hound?

"Emily," Will stood between her and Wit, breaking Emily's trance. Sensing she was still not listening completely, Will made pointed eye contact, "Wit is a vampire—you need to go bathe now to get the scents of your world off of you before he gets hungry or sick." Will nodded as he spoke, Emily's head bobbed along with his, though her eyes kept trying to sneak around him to glance the newcomer. Will had to walk Emily to the door.

Waiting outside was the young man who had been cleaning when they walked in. "Son of Nimble, would you please tell the maids that her Highness would like to wash off the travels. They know how she likes her bath." The young man rushed up the stairs. Will turned back toward the library, pointing at Wit, "You stay. We need to talk."

Wit was still looking as if he needed to lie down or take a walk outside. His handsome, pale complexion had turned a sickly hue while his eyes had become enraged. Emily looked away as Will guided her toward one of the staircases. Even with him out of her sight, and even with her last glimpse of him being so harsh and tarnished, his beautiful face remained in the front of her thoughts.

When she was upstairs, Emily was met by two tall, thin young ladies who looked half-starved. They said nothing and made no expressions while they brought her to a large room with a bathtub in the middle. Steam rose from the tub—scalding hot, just like she used to take when she lived in an apartment with a full bathroom. The ladies tried to help her undress, but Emily stopped them once they loosened the back of the dress, "Please, I would like my privacy today." The maids nodded and left her. After shoving all of the parts of her dress into a pile on a chair in the corner of the room, Emily slipped into the bath.

The water was painful on her skin, but she could never feel clean without the burning feeling. She finally had a moment alone to contemplate. She realized how terrible her interaction with Wit had been—she held her face in her hands while letting out an, "Oh my God" squeal of disbelief of both her awkwardness and his attractiveness. The soap they had left for her had no scent—no peppermint, no fruit, no sandalwood. She washed herself twice over to make sure whatever smell had revolted Wit would be gone. She would not have a repeat of the interaction before. She felt a need to impress him—to get him on her side, at the very least. A vampire could be a powerful ally.

Where her old clothes had been was a new, clean dress. It was a little unnerving, as Emily had not heard anyone enter the room while she was bathing. Thankfully, the wool was much softer than the dress she had worn earlier, but she still would have given her left arm for some cotton. As she was dressing, she saw what she assumed to be a chamber pot in the corner and realized she had yet to need to use the restroom—thankfully. She decided not to ask about it and just chalk up the phenomenon to magic, especially since the only two people she could ask were both men.

The dress had the same parts as the old one—it must be the current fashion—except there was also a sort of corset she would have to fiddle with. She grumbled lightly, realizing she might not get her bra back. She put on the underskirt, followed by the dress which she buttoned to the breastplate and tied up the back in the way Will had taught her. Finally she pulled on the coat. This one only covered halfway down her arm, revealing the stripes on her right forearm. She caressed them lightly. The dress was a lower cut in the chest—it made Emily feel more feminine to be showing more skin. There was no mirror in the room—either there was no vanity in this world, or the vampires felt bad for not being able to see their reflections and had them banned. Many people had told her in the past that she had a lovely neck, so she wore her hair up often. She pulled her blonde hair into a long braid that circled her head like a tiara. One of her friends from work had taught her—she had called it a "princess braid." How appropriate.

Emily took advantage of her time alone. She toyed with magic—mostly telekinetic things like opening the door and bringing things to her. She laid down on the lounge chair. She looked out the small window at the courtyard below—she could not see the city past the walls of the estate, but it looked to be the middle of the night and she could hear the bustle through the thin glass. She heard a knock at the door and a girls' voice called through faintly, "Does her Highness need assistance?"

The hairbrush Emily had been calling to herself clattered on the ground, as the knocking had broken her concentration, "Uh, no...thank you...I'm quite alright!" She sounded unsure and unregal. She composed herself and hollered again, "Let the gentlemen know I will be down momentarily." When Emily said this, her back was straight and her chin was up. Somehow this posture could be heard in her voice—clear and assertive. Emily held this posture and air about her as she made her way back downstairs.

As she reached the bottom of the staircases, Wit was waiting for her with an apologetic look on his face and his hand outstretched to help with the last two steps. He was no longer sickly looking, but back to the stunning gentleman she had seen when he first walked into the library. When he smiled, a slight glimpse of his sharp canine teeth unsettled Emily slightly, but that was offset by how well his smile complimented his features. She was close enough to see his eyes—they were a crystal blue you could only find in glaciers. His voice floated through the air to her, "You must forgive my behavior earlier. I was startled by you being here and by the human smells you carried with you. I hope we can start again."

Emily feigned confidence and smiled back, realizing she had been staring again, "Nothing to forgive—I am quite startled by my being here, as well. It was not by choice, I can assure you, but I will do what I can." She made it down the last steps with her hand in his. His hands were colder than Will's, but her own hand seemed to become warmer to compensate in the places their skin met.

Wit seemed to feel this, too, and held her hand completely in his, squeezing it lightly. He brought his face close to her ear and whispered, "You may be part demon, but you tempt me in a way only a human can." He stepped back and his eyes scanned her from head to toe, lingering on her neck for an uncomfortable amount of time.

"You will need to restrain yourself, then," Emily said coyly, yet uncomfortably at the same time, "As you did with my sister."

She looked around the room only after saying this, to make sure nobody could hear them.

"Although you are sisters, there is something in you that does not exist in her," Wit said. "It may be what is needed for the plan to work."

Just then, Will left the library to join them, "I hope you two have made up. We have work to do." He walked over to Emily and kissed her cheek, "It's me." Will led them back to the library, Wit secretly holding Emily's hand the whole way. Emily was nervous—if someone had seen them, wouldn't they suspect something strange going on? They entered the library and Will continued, "Wit came up with an ingenious idea—we are to hold a ball. Here. We have yet to have an engagement celebration, so that will be the occasion. Someone in the room would be bound to be surprised by your miraculous recovery—and they might have the answers we are looking for."

Emily lit up, but that was quickly followed by a wave of apprehension. She thought back to all of the books she'd read with elaborately decorated halls and carriage after carriage dropping off elegantly-dressed people, but then the image shifted as she realized that all of those individuals would be dark creatures, some of whom wish her—or at least the sister she was pretending to be—dead. She was to be bait, dangled in front of individuals who never knew her world because her kind scared their ancestors away. Her first ball would not be a cotillion or being presented at court, she wouldn't be giddy with excitement; it would be nerve-wracking in all the wrong ways.

They would need time to plan and prepare, so they settled on a week. Emily would not be able to stay with Will during that entire time, as it would be considered a scandal for an unnamed woman to stay overday, so she would have to go to the palace and play her role there. He would invite the guests, but not let them know the reason, so they can be appropriately surprised to find out the news of both their engagement and her presence at the party.

"What do I need to know before I go to the palace?" Emily asked, realizing she was not prepared to impersonate someone among others who know her so well.

"Keep to your room as much as possible," Will said, understanding her realization. "It will be nearly impossible to uphold the facade for long. Minimize your interactions with your father, but you cannot refuse to see him if he calls on you. Your sister's relationship with him is close, but more official than familial—he relies on her for a lot of political work and advising. Just tell him you are busy with arrangements for the ball. He would be happy to see her so invested in something social; she works too hard and too much. I will call on you as much as possible—I will have things to tend to here as well as nightly business that simply cannot wait. I can send the carriage for you a few times for you to relax here when you need to escape."

Wit was resting against a bookshelf looking pensive, like he realized something and wanted to say it but decided against it, settling on "I can also come by if it will help."

Emily beamed, "Absolutely. A friendly face would be welcome in this terrible place."

"Highness, it may not be the ideal fantasyland," Wit smirked, "but it is home."

"Please," Emily pleaded, "forgive me, and call me Emily. I would appreciate if you called me by my name."

"You are the only heir in the region," Wit pointed out, "A princess in your own right. I shall call you by an appropriate title."

Emily longed to hear her name from Wit's lips. She felt as if she could die happy if he just whispered it—like all that mattered in the world was for him to acknowledge her in this small way. Instead, Will and Wit continued making plans. By the time they had finished plotting, it was nearing daybreak. Wit left for home, but not before kissing Emily's hand and once more calling her "Highness."

Then it was Emily's turn. Will squared Emily's shoulders toward himself. He brushed off parts of her dress and ran his fingers along her braided hair—she would later find out he was darkening it to match her sister's brown hue. The same carriage pulled up—moving into the light from the house, she could see reflections of torchlight on the gold decoration that adorned the metal frame. Emily looked at Will with a pleading look in her eyes, "I can't do this."

Will held her by both hands, "You can, and you must. You look the part and I have seen you present yourself with confidence. You speak with authority, and you are tougher than any woman in this world. You are a princess. You feel like you have something to prove being part human in a world that hates you."

Emily wasn't sure if he was speaking about her or how she would have to act as her sister, but either way that is the persona she needed to present. She nodded, her eyes downcast. She was too tired to feign bravery.

Chapter Four

The carriage ride was only a few minutes—and a much more comfortable ride now that she was alone. She needed time to recharge her social energy, and this whole adventure had spent more of that energy than she anticipated. She watched the city as she passed by. It looked like an old European village with cobbled streets and stone houses. No building was more than three stories tall. The stones were not monochromatic, she could see buildings made from all sorts of rock, and some were even painted, but she wished to see just a hint of a grassy yard or even a shrub. The sun was rising in the distance, and the townsfolk all seemed to be hurrying away to their homes. They were so strange-looking, but also very human. Of course, many were very human-like in most of their features, like Wit and Will were, but even those with horns still had two legs, two arms, two eyes, a nose, and a mouth—just with added or adjusted features and colors. Some beings put up the hoods of their capes or draped veils over their faces as they noticed signs of the sun's arrival.

The palace was visible from a distance and Emily marveled at it during their approach. The building's footprint was a U-shape, with a black iron gate enclosing the courtyard in the front. The baroque facade was intimidating in the dark, but as the sun rose higher in the sky, the heavy stone shone with a regal brightness. Day or night, the building exuded power and importance.

The carriage arrived through the gates as the sun's rays could be felt. When Emily stepped out in front of the main doors, she paused for a moment to bask in it and feel the warmth on her skin. The red-haired, stalky footman waiting to help her down the stairs looked uncomfortable waiting for her in the sunshine, so Emily hurried out and into the front doors which were opened for her. The footman followed with a suitcase and asked, "Would your Highness like this delivered to her room?"

Emily was taken aback. She didn't bring any luggage. She realized what must have been Will's plan, "Yes. I will be up shortly." The young man didn't look suited to carrying luggage, having such a slender build, but lifted the leather trunk that was attached to the back of the carriage easily enough. As he entered the building, Emily stayed at his heels. She didn't have much time to look around; she was trying to keep an eye on where the footman was going. She followed him at a distance up the stairs and along a balcony corridor that encircled a great hall. There was one more story above them, which she could see from her vantage point on the second story.

The room and its high walls looked like a museum of art. Every inch of the stone wall enclosing that room was covered with a tapestry or painting. She couldn't get a good look at each individual piece, but her father was certainly a collector of some sort. She got to the door just as the footman was leaving empty-handed—her cue that this was her sister's room, "Thank you. That will be all." After she passed by the young man and entered the room she paused, realizing there was more that could be said, "Please let my father know I have arrived."

The footman reached in to shut the door behind him, "He has already been made aware, your Highness." He nodded his head in a curt bow and shut the door.

Emily sighed in relief—this first ruse of many was a success. She had walked all of two hundred steps but felt like she had just run a sprint. Her heart was pounding, she was short of breath, and a small bead of sweat was forming in her hairline. She leaned against the bed and tried to compose herself.

The room was grand and ornately decorated. The shuttered windows were tall with purple velvet curtains from floor to ceiling to further block the light. Oil lanterns were on each side of the bed and a candle chandelier was hanging from the ceiling, giving the purple of the curtains a warm, soft, and welcoming glow. There were tapestries warming both the ambiance and the temperature of the room, covering the harsh, cold stone walls that boxed her in.

She looked through the closet, which was filled with dresses of all sorts, but most with half-length sleeves or shorter—her sister must have been proud of her markings. They were the only part of her that indicated openly that she was more than just human, like Wit's teeth or Will's eyes. These things would have been hidden before they had their own world, now it is her badge of honor, proof she belongs here. The dresses were nice, but not what she would consider regal. They were respectable and beautifully colored, but not flashy or ornate in the way of old French aristocracy. Emily touched each dress to see if there was a fabric that would suit her. All were wool, though some softer than others. It was the designs that made her consider changing her clothes. While she had many in the same style she had been wearing, with the underskirt, dress, and coat, there were a few simpler styles more reminiscent of a Jane Austen miniseries: an empress cut gown without the frills or bulk of what she was in now. She would need the ease of movement to scope out the palace today while everyone else was asleep.

Emily gave the house a few hours to settle down. She could hear plates being put away, shutters being closed tight against the brightening sun, and voices of the staff laughing as they went about their business. She knew the young, red-headed footman was still downstairs, as his voice she recognized among all the others, though she could not hear exactly what he was saying.

Once no more noises came from the great hall or its surrounding area, she tucked her head out of the door. Her heart stopped when she saw the footman and a young maid standing outside her room. They hadn't been talking or even whispering but seemed to be waiting for something. She committed to opening the door and walked through it confidently, with her head held high. She did a double-take as she passed in front of the two who were standing at attention against the wall. They were an odd couple—though they looked similar in age, the footman was a great deal taller than the petite young lady. While he had fair skin and hair, she was of the unusual coloring that was not abnormal here.

"I couldn't sleep," Emily explained, looking down the hallway but addressing them, "I thought I'd take a turn about the halls."

The young maid stepped forward, "May I escort you, your Highness? Things may be...different from what you remember."

Emily looked at her, unsure of how to respond. She seemed like a pleasant young girl. Her skin had a purple hue to it and she had pitch black hair. She was a whole head shorter than Emily but did not seem that much younger. Her large eyes were human-like, but her irises were a lavender color—a more intense iteration of her skin tone. She had two bumps on her forehead, like the buds of two horns. She remembered the gentleman from the first establishment she visited and checked the young lady for hooves, which she did not have as far as Emily could tell, though the girl's skirt fell nearly all the way to the floor. Emily nodded, "Of course. I would appreciate the company," she held out her arm for the young girl to loop her arm through. She was confused about the comment—how long had her sister been away? "What has changed since I was last at home?"

The young lady took Emily's arm and looked up at her sideways, as if she was looking for clues in her face, "Your Highness, it has been so long since anyone has seen you. Some might say it's felt...like years?" The girl scrunched the left side of her face, almost wincing, like she had just placed a large bet and was waiting to see how it turned out.

She knew. How could she know? She had been here all of two hours and had talked to one person. Could they have guessed so easily? Emily looked forward as they walked together, "I had business to attend to."

"I'm afraid I haven't yet been able to make your acquaintance," the young girl stopped, unlooped her arm, and curtsied before linking back up to continue on, "Daughter of Brawn, at your service."

Emily continued in moderate silence. Daughter of Brawn kept up most of the conversation. She was naming each room they passed without making it into a tour, "I love what your father has done with the Moon Room—I like to go in there when there are no guests staying, but we wouldn't want to disturb the Duke while he is here on regional business. The North Room has also been remodeled, but it seems they are not quite done with the window treatments, so it'd be best to avoid going in there during the day. Oh, and the East Room," she gave a harumph, "That draft always makes it so hard to light the fire in there."

Overall, Daughter of Brawn managed to talk about at least thirty rooms over the three floors, and she gave a general idea of the makeup of the two additional wings. She spoke quickly, but not in a dismissive way—she seemed genuinely excited to be talking about the make-up of the house, or she was excited about the person she was talking to. She didn't make any more inquiries into where Daughter of Champion had been, but she did eye Emily suspiciously more than a few times. Emily felt uncomfortable, but at least she was being discreet if she did know anything.

Their walk took about an hour, but the footman was still by her door as she returned. He had a knowing smile and straightened when they arrived, "Is your Highness feeling more disposed to sleep? Or would she like some conversation to put her mind at ease?"

"As you, of course, know," Daughter of Brawn extended her hand, gesturing toward the young man, "Empath has worked here for years. We started in the same year. Your father appreciated his gift for reading emotions so much that he kept him on even after his trial. He may be the perfect person to help with what you're feeling right now," she paused as if to end, but quickly added, "as he has in the past."

Emily remembered her overwhelming emotion as she left the carriage at her arrival. If he could read emotions, he would have known then that something was askew. Emily needed an ally that wasn't a kidnapper or someone so overwhelmingly handsome that she couldn't function. Daughter of Brawn seemed kind enough, at least to the point she had known and hadn't turned Emily in yet, and Empath had known even longer, "Perhaps a good conversation would help me sleep better. Please, both of you, come in."

When the door was shut, Daughter of Brawn traced the edges of the door and walked to each of the windows to do the same. When she was finished she paused, looking out the window, and sighed, "It's you," she turned to look at Emily, who was sitting on the bed, "isn't it, *Second* Daughter of Champion?" She had excitement in her eyes and seemed to be holding her breath, waiting for a response.

Four people now held this vital information, they could be the ones to cause the plan to come crashing down. Emily could try to deny it, but these two knew her sister well enough; now that they were suspicious, they could easily ask questions or put her in situations that would reveal she was not who she was saying she was, "Yes. I'm Emily," Emily smiled at saying her own name. It was her new favorite secret that she chose to share with someone—somewhat forcibly, as there were two dark magical individuals sitting opposite her in a locked and possibly sound-proofed room.

Empath smirked, "A relief, I'm sure, to be able to say your own name."

Emily hadn't noticed yet, but her shoulders had lowered and her jaw was sore from being so tense, finally releasing enough to feel the ache. The two were still standing, seemingly looming over Emily, even Daughter of Brawn who was just barely the same height while Emily was sitting. Emily indicated toward the lounge chairs that were in the room so they could sit.

Empath continued as he sat, signaling to Daughter of Brawn, who had not picked up on the invitation, "You can trust us. We are loyal to your father and your family." They sat looking at her expectantly.

Emily stared back for a few moments. What did they want her to say? Was she supposed to ask questions? Would he just know what she's thinking? She tested out by whispering *hello* to herself in her mind. No response from Empath. Not a word thing. Good. "How much do you two know?"

Daughter of Brawn bubbled up, excited to speak, "Empath noticed you were very anxious and lost when you arrived. He could tell you were an imposter of some kind—you apparently read very differently from your sister—"

"Easier to read," Empath interrupted, "less guarded."

Daughter of Brawn made a face at Empath which indicated to Emily that they were close friends, like a feigned offense that he would interrupt, "But he didn't read ill intent. He brought this information to me and we came to a conclusion together. I would have never guessed without his reading, though, High-" Daughter of Brawn's voice got quiet and she sheepishly asked,

"Where...is your sister? If she is still here, I would call her Highness, but if she is not I would think you would be called Highness..." she paused momentarily for a response, but instead continued going with her questioning, "When did you get here? And why did you come? Not that we're not happy to see you," she sounded defensive but pressed on, "but this does put some strain on the way of things. Is your sister spending time in the human world? How long are you going to be here? Are you staging a coup? No, Empath would have been able to pick up on that. He has before. He's very good at these things. Of course, your dad would be the only one powerful enough to even get you here. That must have been a fun reunion—"

Empath, who had been sitting stone-faced while Daughter of Brawn was talking, piped in to interrupt her endless stream of words, "He doesn't know. You want him to know but feel as though you can't tell him."

Emily wasn't sure if she enjoyed being read or not. She did like this loophole that allowed her to tell people without actually telling them, though. She shook her head, "We have a plan and that involves him not knowing. It's easier that way."

"Easier for who?" Daughter of Brawn asked quietly.

Emily wasn't sure how that was meant to be taken—did she mean *"Who is this person you are planning with?"* or *"Is it really what is easiest for you or is it just easier for someone else?"* Emily ignored the double meaning and simply explained a bit based on the questions Daughter of Brawn had been asking, "My sister is in trouble. They need to figure out who is responsible. Will brought me here to help him by posing as her. She is...somewhere safe," As she was saying this, she realized it was foolish to give so much information to two people who could easily turn on her. She immediately regretted trusting them so quickly.

"It's not us," Empath stated blankly, as if he was a statue when he was reading the emotion behind what Emily was saying,

"You will have to take my word for it, but I swear I have no ill wishes toward your sister, and Daughter of Brawn," He paused to give Daughter of Brawn a playful smirk, "has no ill wishes toward anybody."

Daughter of Brawn seemed very playful, almost childlike. She looked at Empath with awe, like a big brother who could do no wrong. She gave off a feeling of innocence, which gave validation to the trust she put in Empath. Emily felt safe with these two, safer than she had with Will or with Wit. She unloaded it all. She told them nearly all of what had happened. It was a relief not to have to go into her emotions to tell a full picture of the story, as Empath would add color commentary on her narration for Daughter of Brawn's sake. When she got to the previous night, Daughter of Brawn didn't need commentary to hear how excited she was about Wit.

"Do not be so trusting of a vampire," she interrupted, taken aback first by Emily's foolishness, then by her own impertinence, "I apologize for being so abrupt, but you need to be wary around him. You are part human. Humans are vampire playthings." She was standing now, almost pleading, standing over Emily with an authority that was more intimidating than helpful.

Emily had no words. She didn't appreciate being called a *plaything*. She wasn't anyone's toy. Who was this creature to tell her who to trust? Did she even know him?

Emapth stepped in, taking Daughter of Brawn by the arm, "You've offended her Highness. I think we should go. She needs her sleep."

Emily wanted to call them back, but also felt the pull of sleep. She sat in silence as they closed the door behind them. The sun was no longer beaming through the cracks in the shades—it was well into the sky and would be going back down soon enough. She thought she wouldn't be able to sleep as she laid her head down with a hundred thoughts running through her mind, but she simply blinked and when she opened her eyes, the fire was lit, the shades were open to a dark night sky, and there was someone knocking on her door.

Chapter Five

When Emily opened the door slightly, the small figure on the other side pushed her way through, "You must forgive me for my misconduct last day, but we do not have time for the formalities of it," Daughter of Brawn had already made her way to the closet and was picking out an outfit, "your father has requested you come down to break your fast with him." She looked a lot more professional than last night. Perhaps professional was not the word—Formal? Direct? Cold? Her tone held less whimsy and excitement, "We will need to make sure you are up to date on what he might try to discuss with you." She held a dress draped across her forearms and looked Emily in the eyes with blank expression, her head cocked in impatience.

Emily closed her eyes tightly, grimacing slightly. Daughter of Brawn spoke quickly, too quickly to register completely in the first moments of being awake. Emily threw herself back on top of the bed, rubbing her palms into her eyes so hard she saw spots. She let out a groan, "I understand that you were trying to look out for me, but I wish you could have given me some credit. I know what a vampire is. We have loads of stories about them back home." She let her elbows fall to her sides as her eyes adjusted back to the light in the room, "But if Will trusts Wit, I think we should, too. We need allies."

Daughter of Brawn smiled at her use of the word "we." She came up to Emily with the dress and her tone returned back to its bouncy nature, "Understood. Now, we need to get you dressed. Your father doesn't like to wait." As she helped Emily get into her dress, she revealed the names of the parts of the dress, including the stay—not a corset. While brushing and fixing Emily's hair, Daughter of Brawn told her a litany of notes about her sister's schedule—where she had been recently, how she thought it might have gone, and what was coming up.

"Were you and my sister close?" Emily managed to force out as her deep red dress was being tightened around her ribs to hug the stay that was already restricting her breathing.

Daughter of Brawn paused, "No," she replied, going quiet as if she was going to end it there, but continued, "I'm not a ladies' maid; I wouldn't have had the chance to even get to know her. I'm hardly seen by the family." She stopped, eyes wide, realizing the picture she was painting, "Not to say that she hasn't been kind! It's my job to go about quietly. When she does notice me, she is ever so kind. Being one to roam about the shadows gives me great insight into the goings-on about the house, hence why I know so much." She got the coat for Emily to put on over the dress—the same style as the one Will had given her, though this one was made from a slightly softer type of wool.

"Between you and Empath you must know all of the secrets of the house," Emily noted, feeling the curves of the dress with her palms, wishing she had a mirror to look in. She felt ridiculous, like a dark Marie Antionette if the queen had ever decided to dress casually. She sat on the bed once again and looked at Daughter of Brawn.

Daughter of Brawn smirked, "He does keep me well-informed," she reached out for Emily's hand, "But please, don't sit. We must go now; your father is waiting." She pulled Emily to her feet, made unstable by clunky, heeled shoes. She steadied Emily and looked up into her face, "Are you sure you don't want him to know?"

Emily nodded, scrunching her eyebrows, "Yeah, I mean," she paused, shaking her head and shrugging, "That's the plan."

"If that's your wish," Daughter of Brawn said weakly through a forced, faint smile, "you will need to go down first. Go to the open door under the portrait of the young woman with brown hair. I will be in to stoke the fire soon." She lightly pushed Emily out the door.

Emily made her way down a flight of stairs and paused a moment at the bottom to take in the grandeur of the great hall. The art was amazing—all dark colors, but bringing life into the height of the room as light flickered from the candle chandelier, bringing an illusion of movement. She meandered along the outside of the room, looking at the wall opposite as she went. Eventually her eyes fell upon a portrait of her mother. She was much younger than when Emily had ever known her, she wore makeup, and her hair was not pulled back, but Emily could still recognize her. If she had any doubts about whether or not they found the right person, she knew now. She must have been staring for quite a while, as Daughter of Brawn had managed to catch up to her and give her a nudge forward.

The door to the room was already open, so Emily walked towards it with a whispered "Good luck!" coming from behind. She lifted her head and squared her shoulders as she made her way inside.

The man sitting at the head of the table—the only person in the entire room—was intimidating in size and overall appearance. He seemed almost too large to be sitting in his chair—if it were made of wood, it would have easily collapsed beneath him. His muscles were hardly contained in his suit, which must have been custom made to begin with. His skin was not tinted with an inhuman color, but was streaked with black stripes like his daughter, though his stripes tattooed his bald head, face, and even his hands, which were thumbing through small metal bars inscribed with words. As he finished each one, he wiped the engravings clean with his thumb and discarded them into a pile to the side of his place setting with a *clink*. He didn't look up as he addressed her, "What took you so long?" His voice was as deep and hoarse, yet pleasant.

Emily went directly to the long table at the side that was filled with food and began to serve herself. Conveniently, she got to face away from the menacing figure as she responded, "I was feeling unwell from my travels. I needed time to collect myself." She took some small red potatoes and a hard-boiled egg. She wished for some fruit, anything sweet, really, but knew that would be impossible. She wondered how common scurvy was in the region. On the topic of scurvy, would the Seas have some kind of magical pirates? She shrugged this train of thought off. It was time to meet her father. She turned back to the table as a chair next to her father pulled itself out.

"Come sit," he gestured toward the chair, "tell me how your dealings went. These messages from the mountain region have made me uneasy. Hopefully you have better news."

Emily sat and the chair pushed itself in; she tried not to look surprised. She recalled everything Daughter of Brawn had told her, "We spent a great deal of time along the borders. The meeting with the dwarves could have fared better. No concrete deals, but there was productive discussion," Emily blanked on the other meetings her sister had lined up, "Edge was bustling when we visited. Even stepped into the Null for a bit to gauge how things are there. The border was, thankfully, uneventful." She popped a potato in her mouth to prevent her from rambling on. It was bland, just salt, pepper, and butter, but she was thankful for the food.

Her father sat there in silence for some time. He was holding the last metal bar with both hands, "This message here said you never showed up for the meeting with the dwarves." His tone gave no clues as to his emotion about this fact.

Emily took a moment to finish the bite in her mouth, "I was late. Some of the roads were rough. They must have sent that when I didn't show on time."

"It came this morning," He turned to stare her down. "They have called off negotiations."

Emily hesitated too long. "I... I—"

"You were out with her again!" He bellowed as he slammed his fist on the table. The pile of metal bars clinked as they jumped. His entire body was hunched, bringing his face closer to his daughter's, "You neglect your duty as an heir and you neglect your duty as an ambassador! Darkness help me, I can understand, but we have to make sacrifices!"

"I don't—" Emily's eyes were wide and her breath was short. This towering man was accusing her of something, and she had no idea what it was. She was proud of her improvisation up until this point, but now she was knee-deep with no way out.

Daughter of Brawn walked in. Instead of breaking the tension, her presence made Emily even more uncomfortable. Despite Daughter of Brawn being so light on her feet, Emily could hear each step as the leather of her shoes lightly scraped the floor. She bent down near the fireplace and opened a bag that hung from her shoulder. As she opened it, fire leapt out and licked her arm. She reached in and grabbed a black rock that looked to be burning. She squeezed it in her hand and the small orb of fire became a wild fireball. She tossed it into the fireplace and it roared to life. She turned to the table and bowed, "I am sorry I was late, your Majesty. Please forgive me."

"You are both lucky I am in a forgiving mood," Champion nodded at Daughter of Brawn, dismissing her. When she'd gone, he glared at Emily, "I expect better of you, light of my world, but I love you so much." He reached out to push her hair out of her face. His hands were rough as they brushed her skin. Cold, but still comforting.

Emily had imagined meeting her father so many times, but she would have never concocted this scenario in a million years. Every emotion she had ever felt about her absent parent flooded into her at once—abandonment, excitement, confusion, and, somewhere deep down, a surge of love. Emily couldn't help herself. She leapt out of her chair and wrapped her hands around her father's neck. He hugged his daughter, tiny and fragile in his huge, strong arms. Emily held her breath so as not to let out a stuttered breath. Her eyes welled with tears, but she didn't let them fall.

Champion rubbed his daughter's back, "I know this is hard, but you have to be strong. The things you do for the region will be amazing. You cannot give them a reason to take that from you."

Emily wished she could ask questions. Whatever he was referring to could have something to do with her sister's illness. She would have to make sure to tell Will when she saw him again. Emily kissed her dad's cheek and left without another word.

She stopped as the door to the room closed behind her. She leaned against it and finally let out her breath. Her heart was racing as she tried taking in her breath through hiccoughs. She didn't notice Daughter of Brawn come up beside her and nearly jumped out of her skin when she saw her out of the corner of her eye. "Sweet mother of—!" She yelled, slightly too loud, before bringing her voice to a near-whisper, "What the hell, Daughter of Brawn? Want to give me a heart attack?"

She looked confused, "Heart attack?"

Emily's mouth dropped open in disbelief as her eyes went blank, "Of all of the things I've said since I've been here, *that* is the first thing that doesn't exist here?"

Daughter of Brawn shrugged, "You speak in a strange manner, but so does your father. I assumed they were human terms and could usually piece them together. Your sister uses some of the strange terms, too—she learned them from your father, I assume. I wanted to make sure I understood this time because you were asking if I wanted to give you something—I thought I should ask before I try to guess what it is."

Emily shook her head and sighed but refrained from saying "bless your heart"—she wasn't sure how the phrase would be taken here. "It's a way humans die—when we're scared it can make one happen. It is a way of saying you scared me."

It was Daughter of Brawn's turn to give an incredulous look, "*Humans can truly die of fright?!*" Her eyes were wide, "I was under the impression that was an exaggeration!" Her look quickly changed to that of concern, "Should you even be here?"

"It doesn't actually happen that often, just know that I would appreciate seeing or hearing you before you—" Emily was cut off by the sound of metal scraping against the stone floor in the room behind her, "Go," she whispered to Daughter of Brawn as they rushed away from the door.

Daughter of Brawn grabbed Emily's hand and pulled her to the front door. She pushed Emily out in front of her and closed the door behind them. The night air was drier than it had been before and thousands of stars shone above them—more brilliant than she'd ever seen back home. A carriage was waiting on the gravel path that looped in front of the main door. It looked just like the one she had taken from Will's home to the palace. She looked to Daughter of Brawn, "Will?"

"No, but I assume he was sent by Will."

They both looked back at the carriage as its door opened and a tall, fair figure stepped out. Emily's breath was immediately taken away at the sight of him. She looked back to Daughter of Brawn.

Daughter of Brawn's eyes had a look of worry while her lips were trying to smile, "We need allies," she took Emily's hand, "Please, be careful. I don't want to see anything happen to you. I can come with you if you need me to."

Emily held on to Daughter of Brawn's hands. They were cool and very sturdy for their small size, rough with calluses. She gave an uneasy smile back, "I'll be alright." She was fairly certain it was the truth, but she mostly just wanted to be alone with Wit.

The walk between the door and the carriage seemed endless. Emily did all she could to refrain from running toward him. Each step came with a loud crunch of the gravel beneath her feet. Wit was waiting for her outside the carriage with his hand outstretched, waiting to take hers. Emily's body went numb. She developed tunnel vision—everything but Wit seemed blurry. She could no longer sense anything but him. Tension built not only inside of her body, but also in the air around her. When she was finally close enough to touch his hand, the whole world came back into focus all at once.

Chapter Six

Wit was quiet most of the ride, keeping Emily on edge. She was facing forward while Wit's seat faced the back of the carriage, though he was watching out the window the entire way. The moon was shining brightly through the window, reflecting off Wit's sharp features. He kept his lips closed, but still managed to smirk every so often.

Emily shifted uneasily for most of the ride; her dress had several layers that were not comfortable to sit on. She would glance out the window, as well, from time to time in order to keep track of where they were. Each time she looked out, there were fewer lamps lighting the road, fewer homes nearby. They were leaving the city—but where they were going was still unknown. It was only when she realized she hadn't seen a lantern in nearly ten minutes that she began to panic. She finally was compelled to speak, "Where are we going?"

Wit didn't turn from the window, but reached out and placed his hand on her knee. Emily could feel his icy coldness through the dress fabric—each finger a cold knife piercing her skin. Somehow this made her physically less relaxed, but emotionally more calm. She sat up straighter for the rest of the ride.

They came to a stop by what appeared to be a black field—an ocean of darkness as far as she could see. The moonlight reflected off of the glossy surface. Emily could see waves and troughs in the vast sea, but they were not moving. Still wordless, Wit opened the carriage door and helped Emily out. There was an eggy, mineral-like smell to the air.

"A lava field?" Emily asked as she finally realized.

Wit turned back to the carriage driver, "I will call for you when we need to return. Leave us."

The driver, a lanky, pale man with long white hair, stood from his perch on top of the carriage. He gave a long, bowing nod to Wit, and snapped his fingers. Instantly, he was gone. Not a trace of his presence remained.

"Yes," Wit finally responded. He took out black leather gloves from his coat pocket and slid them on as he walked out onto the bed of rock.

Emily hesitated by the road, but quickly realized she didn't want to be alone in the dark and rushed behind him, lifting her skirts to better see her footing on the uneven ground. Her shoes had little traction, though, and she slipped many times. Wit never looked back to see if she needed help, despite her clumsy exclamations and shrieks as she fell. Again, too much time passed without words for Emily to feel comfortable, "What are we doing out here?" she shouted through labored breaths.

Wit stopped, but continued to look forward, "You are juvenile."

Emily came to Wit's side and looked up at him, again taken aback by how stunningly handsome he was in the moonlight. When she finally caught her breath, she rebuked him, "I'm nineteen and have been mature enough to have taken care of myself for a while now. And who are you to talk—what are you, thirty?" A warm wind picked up around them, whipping Emily's hair into her face.

"I am 28 years old. I have been 28 years old for centuries. I will always be 28 years old," He paused, seeming to consider his next words, "Unlike you, I know how to use my abilities because I've practiced with them almost my entire life. Children are dangerous because they do not know how to control their powers. *You* are dangerous because you do not know how to control your powers. We are here because you need to see what you can do."

"I can move things without touching them," Emily offered.

"Party trick," Wit scoffed, "Toddlers can do that."

"What am I going to learn in the next few days that will help me impersonate someone who has lived here her whole life?" Emily had always been good at picking up new skills, but it always took practice—she was hardly ever successful with something on her first try. She brushed her fingers through her hair, combing it out of her face since the wind was tossing it more violently now.

"I have told Will it is pointless," Wit looked Emily in the eyes, speaking almost in a low growl, "you will be found out. He has unwarranted faith in you—a desperate hope that you will save your sister. A last resort. Your sister was weak enough to fall prey to a curse or a sickness or, if not those, whatever it is that ails her. She was young and weak and distracted by emotion. You are young and weak and inexperienced."

"I get it, I'm new to this," Emily could feel the wind start to pull at her skirt, which acted almost like a sail, trying to pull her in all directions, "But you don't have to be an ass about it."

Wit seemed unaffected by the wind, not even his hair lost its overall shape with only small wisps giving way, "Your human blood will hold you back. Even if every creature accepted you, forgetting the history of your kind hunting down our kind, you still would be half powerless. You may feel I am being insensitive, but you are too sensitive. Notice how much the truth upsets you."

Emily's clenched hands and jaw were obvious signs he was right, but he was crossing a line—did he need to barrage her with this truth? "What's your point?" Her entire focus went into waiting for his answer. She could tell there was now more going on around her, but she stared him down, waiting for his response.

Wit's eyes locked on Emily's, "My point is that you are not welcome here. No human is. In the case of your sister, somebody finally did something about it, and they will do something about you, too."

Emily's face was hot. Her hands, usually cool from poor circulation inherited from her mother, were burning so suddenly she felt needle-like pain from the temperature shift. The low rumble that could be heard before was now a roar that could be felt through her body. The warm wind had stopped but Emily could still feel warmth rising from below her, seeping through her shoes and warming the underside of her skirt, causing it to billow up like it was hooped. "I don't want to be here!" She screamed, louder and deeper than she had ever spoken before, "It is not my fault someone tried to kill my sister and it is not my choice to be here!" One of the troughs under her split, revealing the glowing, thick orange liquid it had been hiding. Emily was startled when she felt the ground give and gathered up her skirts to not get burned by the heat of the lava. Once she changed her focus, the heat emanating from below her began to subside. Her attention snapped back to Wit, the concern in her eyes demanding an explanation.

"It cannot harm you," Wit noted, still calmly standing where he had been though he now stood with one foot on each side of a small stream of fire, "Your ancestors built this world, pulling fire from the seas. They brought their young children to this world during their fits of emotion to create land where there was none, to bring this entire region into existence." He swept his hand, gesturing across the landscape, "Demons have immense power. You come from a long line of strong demons, including your father. Many underestimated him. Therefore, I will not underestimate you." He grabbed her by the chin, pulling her face up to look at him and pushing his finger and thumb into her cheeks, "Now, stop holding back and show us what you can do."

"My emotions aren't a switch," Emily said, pulling her face away from his grasp. As she looked up at him, she noted that he looked confused, "I can't turn them on and off quickly. If anything, I'm confused right now." The dark night was still once again and the orange glow beneath them had almost completely cooled.

"Good," Wit remarked, "confusion is a close relative of anger. We can find our way there easily. Now, tell me all about how you got to this moment."

"Like, right now?" Emily asked with a ruffled brow.

"Yes. Where are you?" Wit questioned, "Who are you? How did you get to this world? What led you to be in this place, here, with me, right now?" He found a place where the cooled lava flow was slightly higher than the rest, using this as a place to sit. He gestured, toward Emily, waiting for her to start.

"Well," Emily hesitated, "I came back to my apartment from a walk and as I was about to make something to eat, someone knocked at my door. When I opened it, a stranger was carrying what looked like a dead body. At first, I just wanted to help the woman, so I let him in, but I now realize how stupid that was. He told me that the woman was my sister and I needed to help. Of course, this was crazy because I was raised as an only child. Then again, now I know different," Emily began pacing back and forth as she was explaining, and the warm wind picked up once again, "or at least I think I know. Then again, this could all be an intricate dream. I feel like comas would have elaborate dream worlds," she sighed, then got back to her train of thought, "So this guy gets frustrated with me and shoves me out the door, but then I just kept falling and woke up in a huge field of ferns.

We walk into some creepy mist. I learn that all the things that go bump in the night actually live in one place and I'm there, surrounded by them. I have to pretend I'm used to it all, but it's weird and confusing and terrifying," Emily's hair was whipped by the wind once again and her words were leaving her so quickly, she was becoming short of breath. Wit, who had been stone-faced, raised and tilted his head slightly, but remained seated and gazing off into the darkness beyond her, "and not only do I have to pretend to be used to it, I have to pretend to be someone else. Someone I've never even met, but conveniently looks a hell of a lot like me. And I'm apparently the only person who can save her! I have to pretend to be someone that someone else wants dead and I need to find out who wants her dead by using myself as—!" Emily was cut off by a hand on her wrist from behind. By this point, Emily had been nearly screaming and was completely unaware of her surroundings. The ground was shaking slightly, giving off a low rumble she could feel in her chest.

A voice whispered from behind, "Feel this," Wit said, almost seductively, "Deep inside you. This feeling is where your power will come from. It is strong, but controllable. Now, think about how unfair this all is. How scared you are. Feel it simmer inside."

Emily nodded, letting her mind linger on the unpleasant thoughts she would normally try to bury. She was facing out into the darkness. The lava field stretched as far as she could see, and small cracks had once again formed on the surface.

"Focus outward, and push that energy," Wit continued, "Throw it before you and cut the earth. You shouldn't be here. They are asking too much of you. You shouldn't have to risk your life to save a stranger."

Emily nodded again. She took a deep breath and fell to her knees. She pounded the sides of her fists on the ground, sending out a shockwave from that point. In front of her, the earth split wide—a river, easily a meter wide, cracked before her, starting from where her hands were still pressed against the ground. The streak of boiling rock continued as far as she could see, illuminating even further than she was able to see before.

Emily decided to try to take it a step further. From her knees, she lifted herself upright, while throwing one of her hands upward in an uppercut. The entire river leapt upwards with it, creating a wall of fire, spitting droplets of molten rock and fire outwards. When she opened her fist, it all dropped back down into its crevice. Emily smirked.

As her emotions settled, Emily suddenly felt lightheaded and weak. She stumbled backward, but Wit was there to catch her with his hands under her arms.

"Your second lesson: magic does not come without cost. It takes a great physical toll, and utilizing emotions takes a great mental toll," Wit lowered her to the ground onto the cloak he had been wearing just moments before. He must have seen this coming. Wit sat beside her and produced a handkerchief from his pocket. He opened it to reveal strips of dried meat, "You must also be hungry after a production like that."

Emily was feeling better now that she was sitting, but realized how hungry she was when she was presented with food. She happily gnawed on the meat until she paused, eyeing Wit suspiciously, "This is...?"

"Pork," he reassured her, "No humans here, remember? I have made do with animal blood for nearly 300 years. Pork and poultry mostly. I would have beef, but my current butler would likely not remain in my service if I went about drinking the blood of cattle."

"Three hundred years?" Emily asked between bites, "So vampires really are immortal?"

"I've only been abstaining from human blood for 300 years," Wit laid down with his hands behind his head, gazing up at the stars above them, "I am far older than that. And yes, we are immortal, so long as we stay away from the things that can kill us."

"How old are you?" Emily picked up the last piece of jerky and laid down alongside Wit. She recognized none of the constellations above them. The stars themselves even seemed to glow differently.

"I was born in your world's 1503," Wit stated, "so that would make me over 500 now. I haven't kept count since my 200th birthday—at some point it does not truly matter anymore."

"You don't even look 30," Emily noted, turning toward him and resting on her elbow. She looked at the side of his face for any clues that he had aged at all.

"You do not age once you are transformed," Wit glanced over to Emily, but went back to looking at the stars, "I was 28 when I was bitten by a vampire."

Emily, realizing they were not going to have a face-to-face conversation, laid back down to stargaze once again, "How did it happen?"

Wit sighed, "It is not a story I would like to share."

"Not sure it is fair that you make me tell you how I got here, but I don't get to know the same about you."

Wit let out a short burst of laughter, then conceded, "My town was conducting a witch hunt. My father was a local leader and I was expected to help. I was sent out to the farms and homes outside the city to question the occupants. One of those individuals happened to be a vampire who felt I needed to understand firsthand what it was like to be hunted."

Emily waited for more, and apparently that was all he was going to say on the subject, as they lay in silence for a few minutes. Emily gestured up toward the stars, "The sky…" she began, looking for anything to say, "It doesn't look quite right."

"These stars are not real," Wit remarked, slightly annoyed, "The sky is but a canvas. Artists paint lights in the sky each night. Only the seven most skilled and honored artists are chosen to

66

light the night—each create the skyscape one night each week," he swept his hand across the sky, dotting an imaginary star every so often, "Sometimes they hide messages or images for us to find. It is beautiful, but nothing compared to the pure power and beauty of fires from far away suns. The planets, as well. None could create something as fascinating as the wandering bodies joining us in a voyage around our star."

"The sun must be real, though. Otherwise people wouldn't be hiding inside during the day, right?"

"The five sisters are the only reason we could ever live in this world. They were from a powerful family of elves rumored to be the most stunning of any," Wit changed his manner of speaking from expository to casual for an aside, "I saw one of them once—in the early days of the building of the regions. She was the most radiant being. I could not look long because doing so hurt my eyes, but I did not wish to ever stop gazing upon her," he went back to his matter-of-fact tone, "These five sisters sacrificed their lives and threw themselves toward the heavens in order to act as a sort of lens through which the sun of your world could fall upon ours. Without the heat or energy the sun provides, most of the other regions would perish, and our food supply would perish with them. We may never see eye-to-eye with those in the other regions, but we all owe a combined debt of gratitude to those sisters."

Emily listened, engaged in the legend until she realized this was the truth—the person telling it was there at the beginning of this world and it was a sort of first-hand account of creation. She was hanging on to every word, wanting to know more, like a child hearing Genesis for the first time, "What about the moon?"

"A beautiful lie," he sighed, "The sun only shines down through the sisters' lens, so it cannot reflect off of a moon. Also, not even this land on which we lie is spherical; creating an entire spherical body to orbit around this slab of land and sea would take centuries—millennia, even. The moon is a part of the art piece designed every night. It is a requirement to have it set before the sun arrives, to warn us of the impending light."

They laid there in silence, admiring the starscape. As the moments slipped by and they both adjusted their bodies to find more comfortable positions on the hard ground, Emily found her forearm lightly resting on top of Wit's.

Emily hadn't realized how tired she was until she was jolted awake from a bump in the road which tossed the carriage she was now lying on the rear bench of. Wit leered and half-chuckled at Emily's confused look and wild hair.

"You hardly ever smile," Emily whispered when her eyes finally found him, "Not really. Or laugh. You smirk. You aren't too big on outward signs of emotion, are you?"

"I would be glad to exhibit emotion in earnest," Wit said, looking back out the window, "but I would not want to make you uncomfortable."

Emily propped herself back up to a seated position, "You don't scare me. I know what you are," she reached her hand out and placed it on his knee, "I trust you."

Wit immediately pulled his legs to the side, slipping out from under her hand, "Humans will say that, but once you see the teeth your most basic instincts tell you to run. I saw you at Will's manor. The fear was plain as day, even if it was only for a moment."

"I was shocked, not scared. I won't run."

Wit turned his head to look her dead in the eyes, "You will. You all do."

Emily was muted by the look in his eye—he has had this talk more than once before. She knew the conversation was over. They sat in silence for the remainder of the ride. When the carriage arrived back at the palace, Wit leaned over to the door and opened it for Emily, not standing. His farewell was a curt nod. Emily wanted to say something more, but she reconsidered and nodded back.

As Emily stepped out of the carriage, Empath was waiting with his hand outstretched. He gave a weak smile, likely in response to her feeling of rejection. Emily could see the moon close to the horizon—day would be coming soon. She faced the palace, but as she passed Empath she whispered, "Long night." She was exhausted, mentally and physically, and just wanted to go to sleep.

Chapter Seven

Emily managed to sleep nearly the entire day. When she woke up, the sun was just setting. She noticed the sun both rose from and set in the same direction. She could watch both sunset and sunrise from her sister's bedroom window. Even though the sun was not truly there, the colors painted in the sky were just as beautiful as home.

As she waited for the night's opportunities to present themselves, Emily toyed with small magical tricks she'd discovered. She practiced setting fire to her hands, which she found very helpful in warming them up. She did some small telekinetic tasks, moving objects around the room, shuffling through her sister's wardrobe. Just as she was growing bored, there was a knock at the door.

"I am here to light the fire, Highness," Daughter of Brawn's voice said from the other side of the door.

"Yes, come in," Emily said with an authoritative tone.

Daughter of Brawn stepped into the room and calmly shut the door behind her. Once the door latched and she traced the edges of the door with her fingers, she immediately reverted into her excitable self, "What happened last night? Empath said it did not seem to have gone well, but you spent nearly the entire night together. He restrained himself, I assume. It's been so long since any vampire has had time alone with anyone with human blood. Typically there were bodyguards assigned if your sister ever had to deal with the vampires. I really do hope Wit is trustworthy—I've always found him so handsome, even by vampire standards." As usual, her words were zooming out of her mouth so quickly Emily had trouble understanding where one idea ended and the next one began.

Emily cut in abruptly, holding out her hand in both a halting and a reassuring manner, "It went fine. He was a perfect gentleman. He wouldn't even show his teeth so as not to offend my human sensibilities," on the last few words, she placed the back of her hand on her forehead in a swooning manner, then straightened back up. "He took me to the lava fields to get out some emotions."

Daughter of Brawn leaned against the post of the bed, cocked her head longingly, and let out a sigh. "I love the lava fields," she said dreamily, "So many good childhood memories with my mother."

"I was wondering about your parents, actually," Emily noted, "I think I met your father in a bar my first night here. Big guy, demon I assume. His name was Brawn."

Daughter of Brawn shook her head, "I am part demon, but not on my father's side. There are scores of individuals named Brawn. My mother is the demon."

"I'm sorry," Emily wasn't sure if this was a faux pas in magical culture, "I didn't mean to——." She paused, now genuinely curious upon giving Daughter of Brawn another look, "But if you don't mind me asking, what, or who, is your dad?"

"A dwarf," Daughter of Brawn giggled, "Demons are not typically made this small. Or this strong. It was a sweet romance, the way my parents speak of it. She went to the Mountains on business and they fell instantly in love. They really did try to make it work, but she did not want to leave her home and he did not want to leave his. The way they spoke about each other, however, I know they still cared for each other. I was placed in the care of my mother because it was easy to control the attributes I inherited from my father, but I needed training in controlling the demonic power. My mom died three years ago and I came to work at the palace. I could have gone with my father, but dwarves do not always take kindly to demons. I also love this region. It is my home. I do go visit my father, though. The Mountains *are* beautiful. Days and nights are the same length, but he lives deep in a mountain so I do not have to expose myself to the sunlight if I do not wish to. They have grasses there—that's why they need more sunlight. And some small trees—I believe they call them 'shrubs.' Green is a lovely color."

Emily was happy to have someone willing to share so much of themselves. Will and Wit both seemed to give plenty of information, but she felt as if she still did not know much about them. Daughter of Brawn was an open book and often offered more than Emily had even asked for. She wanted to continue listening to her ramblings but knew if she didn't interrupt soon the poor girl might run out of breath. "The Mountains sound lovely," she mused.

Another knock came from the door. It was Empath, who had snuck up some food from breakfast, "I was not sure you could manage another meal with your father, so I took the liberty of bringing the meal to you." Emily was not sure how it could be possible, but Daughter of Brawn became even more giddy when she saw him make his way through the doorway.

Emily surveyed the food with ravenous eyes. She felt as if she had not eaten in days. Eggs, meat, and potatoes were offered—seasoned only with salt, but she ate all of it fervently while Daughter of Brawn and Empath made quiet conversation with each other.

As Emily was shoveling another forkload of eggs into her mouth, yet another knock came to the door. She was suddenly thankful she never had the time or energy to change out of her dress from the night before. Emily paused mid-bite, wide-eyed looking between Daughter of Brawn and Empath who both shot back concerned glances.

Daughter of Brawn looked up at Empath and whispered, "Can you read intent?"

Empath placed his finger on his lips, closed his eyes, and nodded slowly. He took Daughter of Brawn by the arm and led her behind the door. He gestured toward the door and nodded, as if to tell Emily it was safe.

"Who is it?" Emily called out.

"Will, here to seek your Highness' advice on the soiree," His voice was cheerier than she had ever heard it.

Emily opened the door wide and gestured for him to come in. Will waited in the doorway and said under his breath, "You must come out, it's not proper for me to come in."

Emily peeked down the hallway, first left, then right. Seeing nobody there, she grabbed Will by the wrist and pulled him into the room.

When the door closed, Will snapped back into his usual serious tone, "You cannot do that. Your father has people who can sense—" He abruptly stopped when he noticed the two figures hiding behind the door.

Daughter of Brawn shrank behind Empath, while Empath gave a half-hearted smile and a wave with his fingertips. Emily noticed for the first time how out of place he looked with his fiery red hair and pale skin. She had seen others with pale skin, but theirs didn't bounce the light quite like Empath's.

Not taking his eyes off of the two in the corner, Will leaned in to kiss Emily's cheek. He whispered sternly, "It's me. Do they know?" before he pulled away.

"My dad has someone that can read minds and you expected me to...what?" Emily realized how upset she was with Will, especially given how relatively well she had been treated most of the night before.

"I was expecting," Will emphasized this word through a slightly clenched jaw, "that you would be able to weave some believable story to throw them off. I was expecting he would be too busy to have time to read you. I was expecting," he again paused at the word, flailing his hands up exasperatedly, "that you would figure it out."

"I can't—!" Emily began shouting, but quickly lowered her voice and stepped in closer to Will, "I can't just lie on the spot—you've given me basically nothing to work with. I can impersonate someone physically, sure, but *mentally*? And how was I supposed to hold a conversation with my dad? He was asking about things I had no idea existed."

"You spoke with your father?!" Will raised his voice again, but like Emily, quickly brought it down to a reasonable volume, "I told you to stay in your room and not talk to anybody. How hard was that instruction to follow? Am I to assume your father knows, too?"

"I don't think so," Emily said, somewhat disappointedly, "He seemed a little preoccupied."

Empath finally stepped out of the corner, "He has no idea."

"There has been trouble in the region, and disputes with the Mountains and with the Seas. I can only assume that is on the forefront of his mind." Will's attention was brought back to the other two in the room, "And them?"

"We know who she is and we know why she is here," Empath disclosed, "I happened to be the one to greet her as she arrived. She made a great attempt in hiding who she was. Do not blame her."

"You will not tell anyone?" Will asked Empath.

"No," Empath stated proudly, "I serve the kingdom and will act in the safety of the princess," He smiled in Emily's direction, "both of the princesses."

Will stepped to the side to eye Daughter of Brawn, still tucked behind Empath, "And this one?"

Daughter of Brawn squared her shoulders and stepped forward, "This one," she said forcibly, "serves the princesses. This one also does not believe it to be fair that one princess should know her father and the other must lie to him. This one also finds your attitude toward this princess to be quite rude." With each statement, Daughter of Brawn took another step toward Will. For her small size, she could be quite intimidating.

"This one," Empath reached to pull Daughter of Brawn back, holding on to her shoulder, "should mind herself when speaking to a demon such as his Lordship." His tone was caring, but firm.

Daughter of Brawn drew her arm up and whipped Empath's hand off of her, but kept her gaze on Will, "This one will not ignore our princess being spoken to in such a manner. While she is here, she is the heir, and someone who is doing a favor for you. I expect you to behave as such." With that, Daughter of Brawn poked Will in the chest and sent him staggering back.

Will's reaction gave the impression that the small poke was more forceful than it had appeared. His mouth was open as if he were going to say something, but he thought a moment longer before he finally coughed and nodded sheepishly.

Emily was finally able to pick up her jaw, which she seemed to have lost control of when Daughter of Brawn began speaking, "Thank you," she managed.

Daughter of Brawn smiled and nodded, glowing a little with pride.

"You came to discuss the ball," Emily changed the subject abruptly.

Will nodded, "I was wondering what dances you knew, so the musicians can prepare."

Emily froze. She would have to dance. How did she not realize before that she would have to dance? "I…" she began, racking her brain for dances she might be able to pull off, "I learned to waltz once in gym class." That was all she could provide, as she highly doubted her knowledge of those numbers played at every wedding and middle school dance would be useful.

The three other faces in the room met her with a blank look. Will spoke up, "I am not familiar with that one. What others do you know?"

Emily smiled wincingly and shrugged her shoulders, "That's kind of it."

Will looked as if he were about to go on another tirade, but Empath took one glance at him, quickly clapped his hands to gain attention, and joyfully announced, "I believe some dance lessons are in order."

Will was startled, but changed course quickly, "Yes. She must learn at least one dance to open the ball." He looked around the room and pursed his lips, "Not here, however. Not enough space."

"We can't very well use any of the other rooms," Daughter of Brawn noted, "someone is bound to walk in on us. It would be very suspicious to see Daughter of Champion learning to dance when it is already well known that she is an accomplished dancer."

"I will take her to my house," Will said, "I do not understand where you two fit into this." Will took Emily's hand and began to walk her to the door. His hand felt cool to the touch, but not as cold as Wit's skin had felt.

Emily put her foot down, both figuratively and literally, causing Will to be pulled back from his forward momentum,

"They will be coming with us. They will help me practice when I come back."

Will said nothing, but growled under his breath as he opened the door and gestured for Emily to leave the room. He did not hold it open for the other two, but they followed a short distance behind.

The group walked quickly through the halls, down the stairs, and to the carriage, so as to discourage anyone from interrupting them. Empath's long legs allowed him to overtake the group and open the carriage door for Will and Emily. He helped Daughter of Brawn onto the driver's chair and climbed up next to her, squeezing in with the driver who was smarter than to ask questions.

Emily and Will were alone, facing each other in the carriage. Emily was looking out the window, but at one point she felt a gaze upon her. She met Will's eyes for a split second before he turned away. She turned back to the window, but occasionally glanced in his direction to see if she could catch him staring again. The ride was short and wordless—there seemed to have been an unspoken agreement that they would not speak again until they were alone as a group again.

They arrived at the red brick house. Emily was once again in awe of it. She had seen the greatness of the palace, but the warmth of the brick of this house and the light of the chandelier through the large windows still captivated her. Will escorted them up the stairs and to the left into a large, empty room, pausing by the door to tell a nearby servant to go tend to matters elsewhere in the house. Daughter of Brawn and Empath followed after the servant was out of sight. All eyes fell on Emily, who was standing facing the other three in this dark, empty room.

"I can't dance," she stated bluntly.

"Of course you can," Daughter of Brawn offered enthusiastically, "You can walls."

"Waltz," Emily corrected, "and you all don't know it anyway."

Empath stepped forward, framing his arms as if offering himself as a dancing partner, "Teach me."

"Oh, yes," Daughter of Brawn became giddy, "Empath is a perfect dance partner. Trust me."

Emily stepped forward to meet his frame. She looked down at their feet and bobbed her head, imagining music and trying to remember the steps.

A glow came from the side of the room. She looked up to see Will lighting a lamp on the wall using flame from his hand. He glanced back at her, maintaining eye contact for a little while longer this time. Emily knew she should look away, but she saw something she hadn't seen in him before. A look that was not as stern, not as harsh as she had seen from him before. A look rooted in his eyes.

She snapped back to Empath, suddenly remembering what to do. Before she could tell him, he was already moving his left foot forward. Emily almost asked how he knew, but then answered her own question. Before she had completed her first box, he seemed to already be leading. His height proved a small challenge, but he adjusted beautifully to fit Emily's height and speed. Before she knew it, they were rotating their steps and gliding across the floor as Empath hummed a tune in three-quarter time. Emily could hear Daughter of Brawn give a sort of squeal of excitement. Just as Emily realized that she remembered nothing more than the basic steps, Empath slowed to a stop to give her time to think.

As she stopped to regain her breath, she caught Will watching with a smile as he paused in lighting the last lamp in the room. One flicker of the lamplight on his face revealed a streak of green in Will's face. Not a sickly green, but a foresty hue that seemed to be hiding just beneath the surface. She would have passed it off as an illusion had the green not been so striking and unexpected.

Empath called to Will, "Sir, let us have you learn the new dance."

Will turned his attention back to the lamp he was lighting, aggressively placing the glass cover back on as if it had been giving him trouble. He approached Emily, matching the frame she presented to him. Empath stood behind him and placed his hands on Will's shoulders to guide him, instructing him, "Left foot forward, right out forward, feet together," as Emily did her part.

After they had the basic step down, Empath left the two of them to practice the footing alone as he took Daughter of Brawn for a spin around the floor while humming the same tune he had before. They were a surprising pair with their exaggerated height difference, but they floated across the room as if they had been dancing the waltz together for years. They excitedly tried spins and dips, some more successful than others, but they genuinely seemed to enjoy dancing together.

Meanwhile, Emily and Will stuck to the basic box step. Their bodies were tense and steps calculated. Emily felt awkward—much like that day they learned how to waltz in the middle school gymnasium. Emily threw her hands down and stopped, "Can you just relax? I can't if you don't. I think this is supposed to be fun." As if on cue, Daughter of Brawn laughed as she was spun once again.

"I am sorry," Will said, "I feel as if I am betraying your sister by dancing while she is suffering. Really, doing anything else feels dishonest as I feel like we are no closer in discovering how to help her."

"We have a plan," Emily pointed out, "and part of that plan requires us to dance as if *nothing* is wrong—as if I am the person you've been dancing with since...whenever you two first danced together." She once more held up her frame and looked at Will expectantly.

He reluctantly met her hands and brought her in slightly closer than he had before. "We met as kids," he stepped off with his left foot, "she was the little girl wanting to play with the older boys. She wasn't the strongest or the fastest, but she was smart. I would allow her to join my team." They were more fluid in their movement now, their feet sliding over the polished stone floor, Emily's skirts gently swaying.

She could feel the shoulder on which she was resting her hand was less tense than it had been before. It still felt a little awkward, but she chalked it up to being an inexperienced dance partner. She hoped getting Will to talk more would settle him further, "And how did little Will get the honor of playing with the princess?"

"Little Son of Strike," Will corrected, "was the child of a high-ranking city official. Frequent meetings between the fathers led to a friendship between them, and thus many opportunities for their children to be together." He looked over to Daughter of Brawn and Empath, then back to Emily, "Let's try that—I step back, you," he placed his hand on her hip, turning it slightly towards their hands that were still joined, "turn out on the second," as her hip turned, his hand moved to the small of her back, leading her through the turn and under their arms, "three, one, together," the completed circle brought them face to face again and his hand found her waist once more, "and back." He smiled upon the successful completion of the spin.

Emily smiled, too, as they continued to practice the basic step. She enjoyed seeing Will smile. It was about time he enjoyed himself, even just a little. She would have been proud of the turn, but she could take no credit for it, as Will had led her through it completely. Now that the turn was finished, they were slightly closer than they had been before. "Try the turn again?" Emily suggested.

Will nodded and led Emily through the steps once more. Each time he repositioned his hand, Emily felt confident in letting him lead her, as if his hand gave her reassurance that he knew what to do and would guide her. Again, Emily felt her body pressed closer against Will's than when the turn had begun. Her breath caught in her chest as she looked up into his eyes. Will's eyes met hers and for a moment Emily forgot herself, rising onto her toes to bring her face closer to his. She realized her foolishness partway through the action, pausing for a moment, then moving in to kiss his cheek. She quickly fell back onto her heels and turned away, just now noticing that Empath and Daughter of Brawn were no longer in the room. She wondered how long they had been dancing without music.

Seizing the rare and private moment they had, Emily turned back to Will and asked, "Why don't you look like a demon?"

Will, whose fingertips had been brought up to rest on his cheek, quickly pulled his hand down and became defensive, "Who says a demon must look a certain way?"

"You look human," Emily pointed out, "you said you have no human blood, but you look human."

"A demon can appear human," Will said dismissively.

"Not the ones I've seen," Emily shot back, "You've talked about people changing their appearance—why do you change yours?"

Will sneered, "I do not."

"Don't lie to me," the sound of Emily's voice carried through the empty room and came back to her at a startling volume, she lowered it once more, "you're hiding something. I saw it. Are you just trying to make me comfortable? You don't need to do that. I can handle whatever you really look like," she paused, considering, "or are you even the person you say you are?"

Will laughed an exhausted laugh, then brought his tone down to an angry whisper, coming in closer to Emily, "You have an inflated sense of self if you think I would change my appearance for you. There are things that are not allowed here, and it is best if others never figure out they are hiding in plain sight." By this point, Will's face was right next to Emily's. He kissed her cheek, lingering slightly longer than normal, "But it is still me—the me who needs your help to save your sister. The me who is going to get you home safe." His cool breath on her cheek sent a chill down her neck and through her arms.

Emily sheepishly tucked away, "You know," she paused, looking into his face and smirking, "green is a very lovely color."

Will smiled the warmest smile Emily had seen so far, his dark eyes were mostly hidden behind his cheeks. He gave no other acknowledgement of the statement. He suddenly looked around the room, confused when he found it empty. With no other cue, Empath walked back in the door with Daughter of Brawn.

"The ball can be opened with a new dance," Empath pointed out, "but you will need to learn at least one other that the rest of the party will know."

"The more traditional types may look down on the new dance; it seems rather animated and unrestrained. We should do a classic dance to counter their disapproval—an English minuet should do nicely," Will offered his hand to Emily, "Have you rested long enough?" Emily smiled and took his hand. He led her to one side of the room and placed their bodies so they were both facing the opposite wall. Empath and Daughter of Brawn stood behind them, also hand-in-hand. "Lead with your right," on Will's cue they stepped with their right, "bring your feet together—we can add more here later, but just the step for now, then quickly left, right, left." They continued this step until they neared the end of the room, "Now we will try the step series twice, but moving away from each other and rejoining behind the others." Once Will released Emily's hand, she misstepped, but quickly shuffled her feet back to the correct step before they rejoined, at which point Empath and Daughter of Brawn did the same maneuver to end up behind Emily and Will again.

Emily turned back toward Will, "This looks a lot more precise," her voice betrayed concern, "how am I supposed to know when to do what without you calling the movement out to me?"

"We will notate the composition of movements and have the night's artist show them in the stars—everyone will practice and come prepared for the same dance," Will reassured her, holding both of her hands in between his, "The party will do others from past balls, but we will not dance those, and you will not be expected to dance with anyone else since you are being presented as my fiancée."

They continued to practice the minuet and the feeling of Will's hand in hers became comfortable. When they parted, Emily would grow giddy in anticipation of reconnecting just twelve beats later. She chalked up the emotion to the excitement of dancing, though deep down she knew she was feeling something she shouldn't. They developed the choreography together and it was written on two sheets of parchment—one for Emily to take with her and one to send to the artist for the next evening's starscape.

After practice, Emily laid down on the cold stone floor. Will and Daughter of Brawn sprawled out with her, while Empath went to find someone to bring food. When he returned, he joined the three lying on the floor. They looked up at the ceiling, which was painted to look like a cloudy night's sky. A large moon was painted just off center. It looked like an opening from an old monster movie. "If the moon isn't real, what happens with werewolves?" Emily asked.

"There are no lycanthropes remaining," Empath replied, "In order to live here, they had to be superhuman in some way. Lycanthropes only changed when the moon was full, but without a moon they were only human. They could not be sent back, however, as it would have kept something magical in the old world. The vampires and the elves both offered choices. The vampires would bite them, thus making them vampires and allowing them to stay. The elves offered a potion that would remove any humanity from them and leave them as wolves for the rest of their lives, allowing them to return to the old world safely. The mountain elves tried a third way, which would have made them fully human, but after some did not survive the process, they no longer offered the third route."

"Empath, you're an elf, right?" Emily asked as she ran her fingers through her warm hair on the cold, polished floor. She enjoyed the sharp contrast in temperature and texture.

"Yes, Highness."

"Aren't you supposed to be hidden away somewhere practicing magic and making potions and stuff?"

"No, Highness. I have the gift of reading emotions, so that is what I was raised to practice, and I must be out among others to refine my power. Others of my kind are expert potion-makers, so they stayed in the mountains to train in their craft."

"You're from the mountains, too?" Emily asked, remembering Daughter of Brawn's parentage.

"Yes, Highness. Many of the best individuals are," his voice became sly and Emily heard Daughter of Brawn giggle from near Empath.

The door opened, but Emily couldn't be bothered to sit up. One of Will's house staff brought a tray of meats and cheeses, setting it on the floor by Emily's feet, and left the room without a word. Emily realized how hungry she was and rolled over onto her side only to see Empath and Daughter of Brawn quickly moving away from each other. She smiled at the sight as she shuffled to the tray.

They laid there talking and eating for what felt like both an instant and several hours. Emily hadn't been so relaxed in a long time. Not even in her world. It had been years since she felt close to anyone at home, since back when her mother had died. She momentarily thought of Wit, wishing he could have been as

84

open as the others, but then brought herself back into the moment.

When it was time to go, Empath and Daughter of Brawn left first to get the carriage ready. When the door closed behind them, Will spoke softly, "I do not wish to hide things from you, Emily," his voice was earnest and warm, "but how did you know?"

Emily walked to him, "I could see it in the lamplight when you were watching us dance. Just a flash, but it was clear as day. From here," she lightly touched behind the corner of his right eye with a finger on her left hand, "to here," she used a finger on her right hand to touch the back of the left side of his jaw. Her hands lingered by the sides of his face. Will's hands came up and gently took Emily's wrists, moving her hands back down. He reached up and traced the path between the two points she indicated with two of his own fingers. In their trail, Emily saw the human skin disappear and a vibrant green painted on what looked like scales that made up his face. It overtook part of his nose and his upper lip. When he was finished, the edges were rough and it looked as if someone had torn the human skin off, revealing a green snakeskin underneath. Emily reached her hands up once again to touch it. It was cold and bumpy, but soft and smooth, like a textured version of his human-like skin. She smiled, "Thank you. I sort of missed the color green." She cupped his face in her left hand and stroked the newly-revealed skin with her thumb. Right as their eyes met, they could hear the metal *clunk* of the door opening. Will quickly turned around to face away from the door, bringing his hand up to hide the part that was still somewhat facing the door.

"The carriage is ready, Sir," the footman announced, then left upon realizing he had interrupted something.

Will was wiping under his eye, as if to wipe away tears, but Emily knew what he was really doing. When he turned back around his face was human once more, "Tell no one."

Emily smiled warmly, "Now we both have a secret," Emily walked to the door and turned back to look at Will just before opening it, "And yours is safe with me."

The sun had begun to rise once again and as Emily left through the main door, she feigned as if she had possibly forgotten something, just so she could stall in the sunlight. When she saw Daughter of Brawn cowering under a cloak, however, she went directly to the carriage where Empath helped her up into the cab, sunlight radiating off of his smiling face.

Chapter Eight

Emily laid on her sister's large and soft bed, staring at the ceiling. She couldn't sleep. The sun was blazing through the slits in the shuttered windows. She would have drawn the shades to help her sleep, but she also missed the light. She felt like a caged animal. She got up to pace. Was it safe to go and wander about the palace? Could she find something to do elsewhere? She cracked open a shutter and felt the warmth of the sun on her face. A light knock on the door behind her caused her to close the shutters abruptly, and perhaps too loudly.

"Does your Highness need anything?" Empath asked quietly through the closed door.

Emily ran to the door and opened it just enough to stick her head through, "I need fresh air and sunlight."

Empath looked down both sides of the hallway, then leaned in closer to Emily, "I believe I know just what you need. Get dressed and meet me by the front door. I have an idea." He hurried off, taking the long strides he could only take when walking alone.

Emily found another high-waisted dress that lent itself more to comfort than fashion. This one was a beige color—she was not sure when her sister could have worn such a light color, but it felt perfect for going out in the daylight. The sleeves were short, so she donned a dark cloak to wear over her shoulders. She hurried down the stairs to the main hall, walking as lightly as she could, though she was never too great at sneaking. Empath was waiting to open the front door for her.

They made their way out to a waiting carriage, as Empath helped Emily in, he said, "You may want to rest on the journey—it will be a few hours before we get to our destination."

Emily nodded and made herself comfortable while Empath drove. She took off the cloak, using it as a pillow. The sunlight beamed in through the windows, warming the square where the rays fell onto her skirt. She was able to nod off a few times, but rose frequently to satisfy her curiosity about what had been out in the darkness. She was able to see that there was at least one river that ran through the region. Along the river were walls and stone docks with boats tied up. Some were filled with goods for sale, but they were covered with animal furs while their owners were away for the day. There were more towns and villages than she had originally thought—the ones she had driven by before must not have had much light, as they had been invisible in the darkness. It all seemed like a ghost town now—not a single individual was outside and the usual bustling noise was gone. All Emily could hear was the rattling of the carriage along the road.

As they progressed, Emily recognized the lava fields off in the distance, stretching as far as she could see. They were not turning to go further into them, however, but drove alongside them, further down the river. She was able to get restful sleep for the last portion of the ride, as she was awoken by the opening of the carriage door.

Empath, who was carrying a wool blanket, held his hand just inside the door to help Emily up and out. As she pulled her head through the doorway, the light blinded her momentarily. As she regained her vision and her eyes adjusted, she saw the sea and felt a rush of salty air meet her face. She took off her shoes and stepped down onto a black sand beach that held the sun's warmth. She felt the grains rearrange themselves, compressing under the soles of her feet and sliding between her toes. He was right. This was just what she needed.

Empath led her to the water, but stopped about midway to lay down the blanket on the beach. As Emily went to dip her toes into the water, Empath got a few more supplies from up on the driver's chair, including a large box he placed next to the blanket. The water was refreshing and cold, but the sun beating down on her back and arms created a warmth she felt above anything else. She stretched out her arms and rubbed her skin as if she were rubbing the sensation in to save for later. She saw the stripes on her arm and stopped.

Empath joined Emily with his shoes in hand, stepping into the water, "If you look out there," he indicated toward a wall of mist that ended partway through the water, "that is the end of this region and the beginning of The Seas. You may catch sight of a siren or sea creature. They're typically the only ones out here during the day."

"Should I worry about one coming to steal you away?" Emily joked.

"No, Highness," Empath replied, straight-faced, "There is much more to them than their power of persuasion. They are very powerful politically. Like the vampires they are immortal, so long as they remain in the sea. They hold great authority in The Seas and find it beneath them to intermingle with the other races, especially from different regions. Perhaps if I were a prince they might take interest, but not a footman. Besides," he looked up at Emily, "I believe you know where I stand in matters of the heart." He walked back to the blanket.

"Actually," Emily started after him, losing her footing in the sand momentarily before she caught herself, "I was wondering about that. You and Daughter of Brawn—just friends or…?"

"She is not allowed to entertain such notions until she is named," Empath sat on the blanket and opened the box, "she will be of age soon enough, and go through a public trial should she need to, then I can tell her how I feel and I can only hope she feels the same way."

Emily sat on the blanket, "Of course she feels the same way. I've seen her when you walk in the room," she peeked into the box to see silk napkins wrapped around foodstuffs, then turned her eyes back to Empath "Can you not," she gestured up and down his person, "just do the reading thing?"

"I am well trained in reading demons," Empath unpacked the picnic, unwrapping a plate of cheeses first, "vampires, too. Humans," he looked unamusedly at Emily, "are too easy. But I do not have much experience reading dwarves. I am told they have strong emotions, but they are well-guarded. I always have a slight understanding of what she is feeling, but never anything deeper." He unwrapped the next parcel, setting it down right in front of Emily.

Emily's eyes grew wide and her heart leapt. Sitting in front of her was a bowl of perfectly red raspberries. "How did you...?" she immediately picked one up, feeling the soft, dry exterior before popping it into her mouth. It was too tart, but perfect at the same time. The sugar went straight to Emily's head and she fell back in sheer bliss.

"Your father keeps them hidden away as a special treat," Empath put one in his mouth as well, "I thought you could use some."

"You thought right. This is amazing." She moved over on the blanket, poised so the bowl of berries was just within her grasp as she lay down. She spread out her hair on the ground, the tips touching the black sand. She soaked in the sun. Empath remained seated with his arms resting on his knees. His sleeves were pulled up, revealing hairless arms glowing in the sun.

"Are you immortal?" Emily asked, popping yet another berry into her mouth.

"Not quite," Empath responded, "but elves do have longer natural lives than humans," he ate a slice of cheese with raspberry on top, "longer than any other creature with a natural life."

Emily sat up to adjust the bottom of her skirt over her knees so her legs could see daylight too. She noticed it had been a while since she shaved. She wouldn't have been so self-conscious if she was not sitting next to an elf with no body hair. She gave a wondering look, then ran her hand over her legs. The smell of singed hair carried on the sea breeze, but sure enough the hair was gone. Emily shrugged, proud of herself, then laid back down. "And it doesn't bother you that you will live longer than, say, a half-demon you might spend your life with?"

"No," Empath was looking out toward the horizon, "I would much rather have her in my life and lose her than never have her in my life at all."

Emily pondered on this and on the limited time she had in her life. She took a berry and used it to trace her lips. The smell of it brought back thoughts of home. The sun, the beach, fruit. She missed it all so much. She was here now, though, and would only have these people in her life for a short time. Then she'd be gone forever, unable to return, unable to contact them, unable to even talk about them to a human that would believe her. Her powers, too. They'd be gone, inaccessible back home. She was determined to enjoy it all while she could.

"Can I try something?" She asked Empath, but before he could give an answer she was already standing, facing down the beach toward the distant wall of mist. She planted her feet deep in the sand and focused.

"Face the other way," Empath cut in, "we do not want to create an inter-regional conflict."

Emily kicked the sand off of her feet and made her way to the other side of the blanket, again digging in her feet. She placed her right hand on the ground, spreading her fingers out and sinking them into the sand, and focused. Her hand caught fire, first red, then a blue flame, and finally white, licking her arm. She could feel the heat from the flame, but no pain to go alongside it. Her hand would not burn. Her arm sank deeper into the sand as the substance below her melted into a liquid. Her excitement grew to the point she could hardly contain it— this was working! The hair on the back of her neck stood on end. Suddenly, she saw a blinding flash of white directly in front of her face. The force and sound pushed her back so aggressively that she didn't even realize what had happened until she was lying on the ground looking wide-eyed at the blue sky. *Where would a lightning bolt have come from?* It suddenly dawned on her as she got up onto her knees and pivoted to look at Empath who, though he hadn't moved, looked equally as stunned.

"Did you see that?!" Emily screamed excitedly, "That was me, right?"

Empath simply nodded, wide-eyed.

Emily squealed, "And I'm not even right-handed!" As she was emoting with her hands, she noticed an electric tingling in her fingertips. She quickly closed her hands and tucked them under her chin to prevent another. She got up and scurried through the sand toward Empath. "Nobody told me I could do lightning. I thought it was just moving stuff and fire and maybe a bit of earth if you count the whole lava thing."

"That is usually the extent of it, Highness," Empath admitted, finally able to speak, "but some demons can conjure other wonders. We did not expect it of you, as your sister does not possess any extraordinary abilities."

"Oh!" Emily exclaimed, running back to the spot she had been focusing on. She dug through the top layer of sand to find a sort of sculpture of glass with sand embedded in it. She pulled it out of the ground and rested it on the surface, appreciating her creation. "Not as cool as I thought it would be," she admitted with disappointment. She clenched her fist for a moment, then flicked all of her fingers out, causing the sculpture to disintegrate back into specks of sand on the beach, "but I can make lightning!" She ran back to Empath excitedly, but slowed when she realized her excitement was not even close to being matched. In fact, the look of concern on Empath's face killed Emily's buzz. "Is this a bad thing?"

"Not necessarily, Highness," Empath said as he straightened the corners of the blanket, "but it concerns me how easily it came to you, and how unintentionally."

Emily sat back down on her spot and grabbed one of the last few berries out of the bowl. After she swallowed she explained, "I was trying to make the sand as hot as I could—I guess it was intentional in that sense. When it comes to how easy it was, I just thought all this magic stuff was easy. I mean, I made a river of lava just by getting upset. It just," she shrugged, "happens."

"It should not just *happen*," Empath informed, "you need to be in better control of it so there are no accidents. It is best not to call attention—" He stopped as if he heard something. Emily listened, but could hear nothing but the wind whipping past her ears. Empath whispered, "Highness, we must go," he began to gather materials and place them back in the box, "Someone knows we are here, and they are very upset."

Emily nodded, helping collect things while shoving the last two berries into her mouth. She hid herself away in the carriage, pulling the cloak over her head and shoulders. Empath threw the box up behind the driver's seat and set off quickly back in the direction they came from.

Empath did not slow down the entire way back to the palace. It was a rough drive and Emily could not get even a wink of shut eye. It was a long drive, which gave Emily time to think. She was more powerful than her sister, apparently. She wanted to tell Wit about this and get his input about her newfound power. She wanted to tell Will, too. Yet, she was not sure who she wanted to tell more. She determined she would discuss this half-demon to half-demon with Daughter of Brawn first. Empath had been concerned about the new power and she did not want either of the other men to be concerned—Daughter of Brawn would be a good litmus as to whether it really should be troubling.

She thought about home and what she would be missing. Her regular day-in, day-out; nothing as exciting as this. Would anyone at work have tried to check in on her after not showing up for a few days? Would they have seen her sister lying half-dead in her bed?

She couldn't think about that now. She had to focus on the task at hand and, perhaps, the present danger. As they approached Capital, rain fell. Emily closed her eyes as she filled her lungs with the smell of fresh rain on dry earth. She was so entranced she did not realize they had arrived at the palace until the carriage jolted to a stop in front of the doors. It was still light, but the sun was just off the horizon—it would set soon enough.

Emily threw open the carriage door and hopped out. All of the excitement came buzzing back in an instant—her new power, someone spotting them, the sunshine, fruit! She rushed to the doors, pulling with the entire weight of her body to get them to open. The entryway and main hall were quiet and sleepy. Emily whispered harshly, "Daughter of Brawn!" as Empath came behind her to take the cloak off of her shoulders. As Emily messed with getting her right arm out from the folds in the cloth, Daughter of Brawn suddenly appeared to her left. As she turned her head back around, she was taken aback and her breath caught in her throat. When she finally regained her voice, she whispered, "One, you need to stop sneaking up on me. Two, we need to get you named, Daughter of Brawn is a mouthful."

Daughter of Brawn smiled sheepishly, "I did not mean to frighten you again. I am so used to being quiet. Dwarves are not very light of foot, so I have to make an effort to sneak about."

"Just warn me if I don't notice you," Emily put her hand on Daughter of Brawn's shoulder, "Okay?"" She turned her attention toward the great hall. Nobody on guard, nobody awake yet, "Is the coast clear?"

"Yes, Highness," Daughter of Brawn took Emily's hand, "but the house staff will be moving about soon. The kitchen fires are already lit and I am going around to the fireplaces now." She pulled Emily up the stairs quickly and threw her into her sister's room just as someone came around the corner. She stuck her face into the doorway and said, "Of course. Immediately, Highness," before shutting Emily in.

Emily turned around and leaned against the door, catching her breath from the sprint up the stairs. Daughter of Brawn had short legs, but moved quickly, she probably took those stairs dozens of times a day. Emily was exhausted after only short bursts of sleep throughout the day, so she laid down on top of the covers for a nap. Curled in the fetal position, she was asleep as her face hit the silk pillowcase.

She dreamed of dancing in the sunlight. She and Will were on a tropical beach and their twirling feet left arcs in the golden sand. She felt Will's hand holding the small of her back, pulling her close. At some point during the dream, Will's face showed the green snakeskin. Emily smiled and said, "My favorite color." She wasn't sure why dream-her said it, as her favorite color was red, but it felt true in the dream. The faint smell of flowers came to her. She felt what she thought was the warmth of the sun on her left cheek, but dream-Will's hand was there. Had it been there before she noticed the warmth? She swore she could feel him caressing her face, stroking his fingertip from her temple to her jaw.

"Wake up," a voice whispered.

Emily snapped from the dream, realizing she did not recognize the voice. The image of Will disappeared, but she kept her eyes closed, trying to process what was real. The warmth on her face was real—someone's hand was there, stroking her face. It was a soft hand, delicate.

"Daucha, I have returned," the woman's voice whispered in a more song-like tone, "wake up. Please."

Daucha—was that her sister? A shortened version of Daughter of Champion? Emily liked it. But who would call her that? She needed to go straight into improvisation mode to pull this off.

Emily squinted her eyes open and smiled weakly. She slowly took in the face that was close to hers—a beautiful young woman with golden, soft curls falling over her shoulders smiled back at her. This woman's hand was on her face. Her brown eyes stared into Emily's and she smiled a dazzling white smile as she saw Emily fully awaken. She pulled away to let Emily sit up.

"Wit sent word that you were sick," the beautiful stranger reached out and fixed a piece of Emily's hair that was out of place, "He was afraid you would not recover—I came as soon as I heard."

Emily followed suit and began to fuss over her hair, running her fingers through it, "I am quite well. I feel as good as I ever have. Kind of you to come all this way to check on me."

"I would have been back in a few weeks' time regardless, I simply cut my trip short," the woman bent close to Emily, who was still seated on the bed. She moved gracefully, placing her hands on the bed on each side of Emily. When she was mere inches away from her face, she whispered, "Besides, where would you be without your Lady-in-waiting to nurse you back to health?" With this, the woman pressed forward. Emily felt the woman's soft, warm lips on hers. Her eyes shot open in terror; thankfully the Lady-in-waiting had her eyes closed. Emily reciprocated as earnestly as she could muster. She couldn't help but note it was a very pleasant kiss. She laid back as the woman pushed forward, but did not want this to progress any further.

Emily placed her hand on the woman's chest and pushed her back, "You know how my father feels about this." She hoped her assumption was correct.

The woman leaned to the side, onto her arm, and used her free hand to tousle the hair from her face, "Of course I do. It has never stopped you before."

Emily sat up in the middle of the bed and crossed her legs, "You're right—I'm sorry. There is a lot on my mind at the moment. Between falling ill and planning a ball for the engagement," Emily eyed the woman's face at the word *engagement*, but it revealed nothing, "I have been in a haze."

"Am I to assume I will not be invited to this ball?" The woman asked with a pout to her lip. As aggravating as that facial expression was to Emily normally, this woman was so beautiful she made any facial gestures look graceful and attractive. Her soft features glowed, much like Empath's face, but more sun-kissed.

"You assume correctly," Emily scooted to the side of the bed, "I cannot have both you and my fiancé making eyes at me all night." She stood and turned to face the woman, who was still lying on her side.

The woman scowled, still in the most lovely manner possible, "Do not lie and pretend your engagement is anything more than the sham it is. Not to me." The woman slid from bed and approached Emily, pointing her finger in an aggressive way, "You can pass it off to the entire world that you two love each other, but you will *not* stand here and tell *me* that you two are anything more than friends."

Was it really a facade? Was her sister really in love with this woman and not Will? Did Will know?

The pause was too long. The woman made her first unpleasant face—her eyebrows slanted sharply downward, creating a sharp crease in her forehead. Her hair rose off her shoulders and began to float as if gravity had stopped working. She looked Emily in the eyes and said, in a sharp but song-like tone, "Kiss me."

Emily looked back, concerned. She did not want to kiss this woman, but if she didn't, she feared she would figure it out. Should she tell her? Her sister obviously trusted her.

Before Emily could bring herself to do anything the woman's eyes widened in shock. Her features softened instantly, but worry spread to her whole face. She whispered something, then repeated it slightly louder, "Imposter." She bolted to the door and opened it before Emily could stop her. She screamed into the hallway, "Imposter!" The word echoed through the hall. The woman smirked back at Emily, crossing her arms in front of her, "Let us see what His Majesty does with those who impersonate the princess."

A clattering of footsteps could be heard in the hallway, but one set shook the ground with every step. As he approached, Emily could hear his deep voice growling, "Out of my way! I will deal with this!" She could see his shadow overtake all of the lamp light from the hallway. He faced the woman, "Where?"

The Lady-in-waiting simply pointed to Emily. Champion's eyes glowed red. He grit his teeth and said, "Everyone stay out. I will handle this." As the woman shuffled out the door, Champion slammed the door behind her. He turned his whole body toward Emily. He hunched over to bring his face to her level, somehow making him appear even more massive and intimidating. Emily could feel the heat from the fire in his eyes. She held her hands in front of her face to block the light. She heard him growl, the sound coming closer slowly, until he whispered from just in front of her "What is your name?"

Emily knew this was her chance to tell him, but she had heard the door creak open—someone in the hallway was listening. Possibly more than one person, or even the whole palace staff. She would try once more, "I am unnamed." She tried to sound confident, but her voice faltered, almost crying. She brought her hands down to her sides and straightened her posture—her sister would not cower.

The large demon's skin began to glow red with fire, "Liar!" His voice boomed, shaking the entire room. He picked up the chair that was next to the bed and threw it behind him. The metal flew across the room, clattering and screeching against the stone floor as it hit the ground in the far corner. Emily was overwhelmed by the noises. The windows unshuttered themselves and flew open. Wind came whipping into the room. She could hear the rain falling hard outside; it was a calming noise, relative to the chaos in the room around her and the clamour from the hallway. There were shouts and calls coming from the crack in the door, but one familiar voice stood above them all shouting, "Your Majesty, wait!"

Champion was in a frenzy. He couldn't hear the voice—he was focused on Emily. He grabbed her hair and pulled. Emily's head jerked back with it. She winced in pain and reached for her scalp, only able to make a squealing sound. Champion lowered his mouth to her ear and whispered, "Tell me who you are and what you have done with my daughter." He pulled his fingers together, adding more tension to the back of Emily's head.

Again, Emily could hear the voice shouting above all the others, "Your Majesty! Wait!"

All she could do was try not to scream. No words came to her lips, which were parted trying to breathe through the pain. She could only look up at the ceiling through the tears that were forming. She was forced onto her tiptoes as her back was arched in a contorted position. She had to say something. She had to startle him out of this, and she felt only the truth could be shocking enough. She shrieked in a whisper, "Emily!"

She was right—his grip loosened, but he still had her firmly as he growled, "How do you know that name?"

Emily could turn her head slightly. A lovely, sly smile could be seen from a crack in the doorway, but it was quickly pushed out of the way as Empath collapsed into the room. The interruption was enough to break Champion's concentration. He let go of Emily and turned as Empath collected himself off the floor.

Emily, too, had to pick herself up after Champion dropped her. She climbed the bedsheets to bring herself upright and when Champion again turned his attention toward her, she said, "You asked my name. I said it."

Champion again turned to Empath, seeking validation.

Empath closed the door, much to the dismay of the peeking faces on the other side. "It's true, your Majesty," is all he said as he caught his breath from what was likely a vigorous push through the crowd collected outside the door.

Champion stomped to the door, opened it, and yelled, "Leave!" before slamming it. He turned back to Emily and approached her slowly.

Emily finished getting to her feet and dodged past him, beelining toward Empath. She wrapped her arms around him and all of her emotions came flooding out. She cried a deep cry and buried her head in Empath's chest, releasing the confusion, fear, and pain she had been bottling. She stayed there for what could have been seconds, minutes, or even hours, but when she collected herself, she looked behind her to see her father sitting on the bed with his head in his hands. She wiped her eyes, hiccoughed back her last sob, and walked up to her father, stopping just out of reach, "Hi. I'm your daughter, Emily."

Chapter Nine

The mood shifted throughout their conversation. It started with her father apologizing profusely for attacking her, then Emily apologizing for lying to him, making sure he knew that she wanted him to know. That was quickly followed by rage when it was revealed that Empath knew she was his daughter and was keeping the secret. Emily had some choice words for Empath, as well, when she confronted him about not telling her about her sister's girlfriend.

Sadness and anger were the next emotions, when Champion asked how her mother was. The way he asked was so hopeful and full of care. There was no way he could have known she had died. Telling him brought Emily back to all of the feelings of loss—she never had anybody to talk to about her mother's sickness and death. Champion held his emotions together until Emily revealed that she had to sell the bookshop. He was furious he couldn't be there to help—he felt terrible that Emily had to handle this all on her own. As much as Emily resented him for not being around, she sympathized that perhaps, just maybe, he really wanted to be there but couldn't.

At some point during the conversation, Empath snuck out of the room. Champion and Emily were deep in conversation about her childhood and her mother. It was nice to have someone else to remember her with.

Finally, Champion asked, "Is your sister in your world? Did she set this up to..." he didn't finish his question, but still waited for an answer.

Emily shook her head and looked at her hands in her lap, "She's been cursed or something. Will took her to my world and asked me to pretend to be her so we could figure out what happened. She's in a sort of dead sleep."

Champion's eyes glowed red once more, "Will? He hid this from me? That fool has been on thin ice as it is. He is supposed to protect her!" He was standing and his voice was starting to boom once again. He paused, shut his eyes, and took a short breath. He sat and opened his eyes once more, "What else do I not know?"

And so it happened that Emily had to once more fill someone in on the plan. She told him everything—except when she got to the part about practicing her powers at the lava fields, she did not mention who it was that took her. Her omission seemed like a good decision when her father asked her, "And Will trusts Wit? Vampires can be powerful allies, but you can never be sure they are actually on your side. You live long enough and you start to believe the only ones who matter are the ones who will still exist in three hundred years."

"Yes, Will trusts him," Emily fidgeted with her fingers, "And I do, too, if that counts for anything."

Champion took Emily's hand in his, "Of course it does, but please be careful around him. Human blood can make a vampire's mind short circuit."

Emily smiled at the metaphor. Without a doubt, her dad had picked that phrase up from her mother; she lived in metaphors and idioms—likely a side effect of spending nearly every waking moment in a bookstore.

"Now that you know, you can help, right?" Emily asked. "You can get the right people involved and help us figure out who did it."

"I am afraid I cannot. The plan as it is currently structured needs me to stay out of it. I distance myself from your sister publicly. She needs to earn a name for herself and make her own decisions. If I am to suddenly take an interest, and to pull away from regional matters that still demand my attention, it will raise suspicions."

Emily deflated. This adventure could have been the opportunity to learn more about her father, but he would not be there by her side. He had to keep up his appearance of being too busy to parent. In fact, he probably was too busy to parent. At least Emily's mom had always been there when she needed her; Daughter of Champion might not have had that luxury with their father.

"Let me teach you something," Champion said, "just to make me feel better about you being out in our world." He rose to close and lock two of the four tall windows. He brought Emily to the window closest to the foot of the bed and tapped on it twice. He then went to the window closer to the headboard and tapped on it twice. The final tap made the glass ripple like a drop of water in a still pond. He then propped his foot onto the window ledge, lifted his body up, and threw his body through the window. Before she could worry, Emily heard a *thump* behind her as he fell to the ground by the foot of the bed. He stood up and said, "A little clumsy, but it can get you out of some tough situations. Always keep one pane of glass active, then use any other pane of glass to return to it. And if you use it," he knocked on the window he just came through, "you will have to re-activate it before it can be used again. You try."

Emily tapped the window by the foot of the bed twice. She went to the window by her pillow and tapped on that one once, twice. The ripple went from where her finger touched to the edge, but did not bounce back—the glass appeared completely normal once again. She was shocked that this would work so easily, on her first attempt. With one finger outstretched, she reached her hand slowly through the glass. It felt wet and cool. She could see her own hand on the other side of the room. She pulled her hand back, then reached through again. She did this multiple times before her father cleared his throat. Emily kneeled on the window frame and pushed herself through the glass. She instantly fell to the floor on the other side of the wall. When she got up, she tried to push her hand back through the glass but stubbed her finger instead.

Champion smiled, "Your sister is very logical. She uses magic differently than I do. She has to think through things and analyze her emotions. But me, I just go for it and let my emotions guide me." He placed his hand on Emily's shoulder. "You are like me, it seems. Feel your emotions and use them, but do not be afraid to do what comes naturally. That is where our power lies."

Emily's mind shot to her sister and portals. She thought of Will, her sister, and her world—where there was no magic. "Do curses work in my world?"

He looked confused, "I suppose small ones may work, but there is not enough magic left there for anything too great. I had to bring potions with me to have enough magic for the return portal when I visited."

"But if someone was cursed here, would it stay with them if they went to our world?" Emily questioned.

"Not for long," Champion's eyes relaxed as he realized where this line of questioning was coming from, "Curses are external forces."

"But a potion," Emily stood up now, "that would stay with someone."

"If your sister ingested a potion of some sort, then she could still be under its effects in your world—a curse would have worn off," Champion rose with her, but was interrupted by a knock at the door.

"Your Majesty," an official voice called through the door, "you are needed for your next appointment."

Champion looked to Emily, took her hands, raised them to his lips, and kissed them, "My baby girl, home again." He smiled. Though his face was still massive and intimidating, it was as soft as she'd ever seen it, "You work this out with Will. I will help when I can, but we have to keep the ruse to secure your plans." He kissed her hands one more time before taking a deep breath and going to the door. As he opened the door, a guard peered in, eyeing Emily. Champion, without facing the guard, said "I am not sure what that woman was on about. That is my daughter. I am sure of it. Be sure the household staff knows this." The door closed behind him, but not before a familiar face snuck in unnoticed.

"Highness, are you alright?" The short, purple figure made her way directly to Emily, "Empath told me what happened. Are you hurt?" She reached to check the back of Emily's head.

"I'm fine," Emily also reached to massage her scalp—it did smart a little, but she would be fine, "I think I just need a bit of rest. It's getting close to day, right?" She did not believe they had been talking very long, but the moon was on its way back to the horizon.

Daughter of Brawn nodded, "I can wake you when it is dark, if you would like."

"I may need someone to fix my hair tomorrow, too. I will need to see Will about a new thought I've had once I am up."

"And you want to look nice when you see him?" Daughter of Brawn asked suggestively as she pulled a sleeping gown from the closet to lay on the bed.

"No," Emily stated very matter-of-factly.

"Or is it Wit you wish to impress?" Daughter of Brawn paused to look at Emily's face.

Emily's eyes got wide and surrendered a bit of emotion, "No!" She said a little more playfully.

Daughter of Brawn went back to her work, "Either way, they both won't be able to keep their eyes off of you." Emily's hand hid her face in embarrassment, but she smiled giddily—how ridiculous it seemed to even be entertaining this conversation. The small demon held up her hands as if she had nothing more to say. She left Emily alone in the room.

Emily fell asleep to a dreamless sleep the moment her head hit the pillow. In what felt like an instant she was waking up to a knock on the door.

When she entered, Daughter of Brawn dropped her bag next to the door and took out a hairbrush. She picked up the chair that Champion threw, which was still on its side in the corner of the room, and led Emily to sit in it. After brushing out the knots, she began to braid Emily's hair, which she then weaved into a braided crown. When she finished, she dropped her hands and let out a sharp breath, "A fine job, if I say so myself."

"And I'll have to take your word for it," Emily felt her hair to help paint a picture of what it looked like. What she wouldn't give for a mirror right now. Mirrors. Glass. Emily quickly scurried to the window and tapped the glass twice before she was helped into a clean, sapphire blue gown. As Daughter of Brawn tightened the laces in the back, Emily remembered something she had been wanting to share, "I conjured lightning."

Daughter of Brawn paused in her pulling, which she did while bracing a foot against the bed frame, "Intentionally?"

"I was trying to make something very hot," her tone shifted from excitement to disappointment, "but was not specifically trying to conjure lightning," she paused, "so, kind of? I guess?"

Daughter of Brawn haphazardly finished tying, and Emily was glad she was distracted—the stay was already tight enough and she found breathing rather nice.

106

Daughter of Brawn began to tidy the room, "What were you feeling?"

Emily sighed and smiled, "I was happy. I was really, really happy. Empath took me to the beach. I was out in the sunshine, eating fruit, talking. I hadn't been that relaxed in ages."

Daughter of Brawn's head lowered, "As long as it wasn't reactive, then it should not worry you," there was a hint of disappointment in her tone. She began to make her way quickly to the door, "I will ask someone to fetch the carriage."

"Wait," Emily reached and touched Daughter of Brawn's arm lightly.

Daughter of Brawn turned and looked up at Emily, her eyes lightly teary.

Emily smiled with pity for the poor girl, "He likes you, you know. He's counting down the days until you're named."

Daughter of Brawn gave a half-attempt at a smile back, "But until then we both have to pretend we are only friends at most. When you leave, there will be no excuse for us to spend time together anymore. Perhaps we will get a stolen moment, but no dancing, no long conversations, no excursions outside of the palace walls."

"But you'll have a whole lifetime!" She threw her arms out wide in exaggeration. She became lost in thought for a moment, bringing her hands together to pick at her own nails before adding on, "Some of us only have a few more days."

Daughter of Brawn's face became serious and her voice dropped quiet and low, "If your sister…" she began, paused to reconsider, then doubled down, "If your sister does not survive, you could stay."

Emily looked at her in disbelief, "What? No…" she stammered out, "She… No… What?" All the while, she realized it was true. If her sister did not recover—if she died from whatever sickened her or stayed in some eternal sleep forever,

Emily could stay. She pushed the thought from her mind, "Not an option. She'll live."

Daughter of Brawn nodded and left, giving a weak half-smile.

The thought stayed with her the entire ride to Will's house. She couldn't shake those three words: You could stay. *You could stay.*

Every little girl grew up wanting to be a princess. Wanting to be swept off their feet by a tall handsome character. Those were the books she grew up with, the movies she watched. Those are the childish dreams she thought she had grown out of. It was all happening, and she could stay to experience and live it all, but at what cost? She didn't even know her sister. It's not as if she owed her anything. But the idea of just letting her die or even hoping that she would die made Emily nauseated. She opened the window of the carriage to let in the cool night air.

She tried to focus on the things she missed from back home. Her mom, who wasn't there anymore. Their apartment above the bookstore, which wasn't hers anymore. The friends she had, who she had lost touch with when she started having to work so hard just to make ends meet. She tried to figure out one thing that was still hers that she wanted to get back to. Her mind kept going to the sister lying in her bed that she wanted to meet—the sister who would leave the moment she got back. The sister who knew what it was like to grow up without one of her parents. The sister she couldn't let die.

You could stay.

Chapter Ten

The short drive felt like an eternity. With the idea of being able to stay, Emily was afraid she would pull back. She would do something half-heartedly. She would hesitate at a crucial moment. She knew she had to commit to something. Above all, she promised herself that she would do everything in her power to save her sister. Whatever else happened, whatever other plans she might concoct, it had to be with the primary intention of saving her sister.

Emily's train of thought ended as she arrived at Will's and was helped out of the carriage by one of Will's house staff. She recognized him. She paused when her feet were on the ground, about to ask the footman's name. She decided against it, realizing it would be a major red flag if her sister already knew him. She would ask Will later.

When she stepped inside the entryway, the room was decorated with glass—even more so than before. An assortment of crystals, suspended in mid-air, refracted firelight around the room. Her eyes, drawn up by the crystal snow, came to find the ceiling was dark as night—as if there was no ceiling at all. The darkness felt cold and endless.

She didn't realize how long she had been staring until she felt someone come up behind her and kiss her cheek, "It's me." Emily closed her eyes and smiled. His hands were on her arms and, although they were cold to the touch, her core seemed to radiate heat that spread through her entire body. She turned to find him looking up. "An artist will be in tomorrow so we can have an indoor starscape for the ball," he noted, "it does look quite empty up there." He turned his attention back to Emily, "What do you need?"

Emily suddenly felt like she needed to know if Will truly loved her sister. She pushed it from her mind because that didn't matter right then. They were close friends. They were engaged. That is all she needed to know about their relationship. "We should start with privacy," Emily gestured toward the library. Will held his arm in that direction to allow Emily to go first. When Will shut the door behind them, Emily suddenly remembered why she had come and nearly exploded, "You could have told me my sister was in another relationship!"

Will's eyes became wide and his hands lightly covered his mouth. After a few moments, he finally brought his hands down to speak, "She had left Capital to be with her family. She was upset when your sister told her of her intention to marry. I thought she would be gone longer, at least long enough to resolve all of this before she returned."

"She came back because she knew my sister was sick," Emily racked her brain, trying to remember how she had known. She snapped a few times as it was coming to her, then exclaimed, "Wit! Wit told her the princess was sick. She came back to take care of her or something." Simply telling Will the information helped cool her temper. Her yelling tapered off.

"Does she know?"

"She knows I'm not my sister," Emily went to sit in one of the large chairs, picking up a leather-bound book from a side table to thumb through so her hands would have something to do. "She made sure to tell my father that much. He was *not* pleased." She stopped on a random page and noticed the book she picked up was not in English; it was not even in a Latin alphabet. She vaguely recognized the characters but couldn't quite tell what language it was. She didn't look up from the book, "She left before my dad found out the truth."

Will was quiet for a while longer before he finally spoke, "I said I did not want him to know, and it was the truth when I said it," his tone was apologetic and somewhat relieved, "but I realize how unfair it was to ask that of you. I was too stubborn to tell you I was wrong, but I am glad your father got to meet you."

"Mm," Emily pressed her lips together. It was not the response she was expecting. Although she did not want to acknowledge his pseudo-apology, she also wanted to sit with it for a while. She kept staring at the unreadable characters in front of her, seething because his stubbornness had created a situation in which she had feared for her life at the hands of her father. Will grabbed something off of the shelf and sat in a chair close by. They both thumbed through their books in silence for at least twenty minutes. Finally, Emily felt ready to speak again, "He and I talked. He is staying out of this whole business with my sister to keep appearances. It is still up to us." She spoke dryly. She was done with the silence, but she wasn't quite done with being upset.

"He should not trust me," Will also kept his eyes on his book and his voice shook slightly as he spoke, "I let one daughter get cursed in the first place and kept his other—"

"Not cursed," Emily interrupted, "a curse would have broken when you came to my world."

Will took his eyes off his book and stared at Emily, "A potion."

"That's what I would assume, my father said he couldn't use magic when he got to my world. He used potions to portal back with my mom. How did you get back?"

"A sort of timed delay," Will stood up to look for another book, but continued speaking with his back turned to Emily, "That's why I had to rush you to get you here—if we did not leave just then, we would have all been trapped there." He stepped on a stool to reach a book on a high shelf. The gold lettering on the front shone in the lamplight as he pulled it down, "Most potions are created by elves. If we can figure out what type of potion it is, we may be able to find out who created it."

"What about a kiss?" Emily cut in.

Will closed the book he had begun to thumb through, keeping a finger tucked in the page he was on. He slowly turned to stare at Emily with reluctance in his eyes, "I am not sure that would be wise."

Emily, realizing she should have included some context, felt a hurt she did not expect and quickly stumbled out her meaning, "If you or her girlfriend love her, she can be cured with a kiss, right?"

Will relaxed his shoulders and chuckled lightly, "That…" he laughed a bit louder, "is not something that works against magic." He lifted his hand to cover his smile, which Emily took to be commentary on her naiveté. He opened the book again and brought it to the chair by Emily, "Besides, I am not sure your sister loves Belle in that way, and I am almost certain Belle is only with her for status and power."

Emily realized that Belle was the perfect name for that woman. Even if she had the most amazing powers or skills, the first thing you would notice about her was her beauty and allure. Emily wanted to stand up for the woman, "Why would you assume she was in it for the power?"

"She is good friends with several vampires," Will was half-focusing on what he was saying while his finger traced down each page. He dog-eared some pages, which made Emily smile since she did this to many of her favorite books. Her mother always scolded her for it, but she couldn't help it. He continued, "Belle and Wit are incredibly close."

Emily's smile disappeared instantly when she heard their names together. She felt blood rushing to her face and heard a pounding in her head. A small part of her knew this was an overreaction, but her mind had already decided it would be upset. She stood up and paced the room as she tried to talk herself down. *Belle is with my sister. She and Wit are likely just friends. I have no possession of Wit. Wit is not even the one I dreamt of earlier. Not that that even matters, because there is no point in even considering a relationship with anyone while I'm here, regardless of how incredibly tempting the prospect is. I am here for my sister. I am here for my sister.*

Emily took a deep breath and checked in with herself. Her heart rate was steady and slowing, her cheeks were cooling down. She went back to sit by Will, who was about halfway through the book.

He paused and showed her the page he was opened to, "I've found a handful of potions that cause a sleep like the one she was in—most are created by elves in the mountains, a few by dark elves, and, strangely enough, one by light elves."

Emily took the book and read the page he had open in front of her:

The Vengeful Sleep—*an elvish potion created from various herbs, spring water, the hair of the one to be put to sleep, and the blood of one who seeks revenge. Brewed deep in underground caverns, the potion takes two days to prepare. Must be finished with an elvish incantation by a higher-level potion master. Can be combined with beverages but will no longer be effective in alcohol. If not reversed within 14 nights, the sleep will become permanent until the sleeping human dies, typically of starvation.*

Emily looked up at Will. He stared back. She whispered, "Are they all like this?"

Will nodded, not breaking eye contact, "Different ingredients, but they all lead to death if not reversed. Some would have her dead already, others give her up to three weeks, but most are around two weeks."

"How long has she been under?"

"Wit found her two days before I came to get you—it took me some time to figure out a plan and research portals, but thankfully your father had an entire collection of books on the topic in his library or it would have taken longer."

Emily fiddled with her fingers, counting, "So two weeks would put us at two nights after the party?"

Will nodded again, "We either have to locate each elvish clan that creates these potions and find antidotes, or we have to figure out who did it the night of the ball and get the answers from them."

Emily knew Will was waiting for her to offer her opinion, but she did not want to give it. Either way she chose, if her sister died, she would always worry that something clouded her judgement—that she intentionally sabotaged the plan. "What should we do?" she asked Will, putting it entirely in his hands.

Will pinched the bridge of his nose and leaned back in the chair, "I have no idea. I am not the one who usually makes decisions. Your sister is much more proficient in choosing the right path forward." He moved his hand, looking up at the ceiling, "What should we do?"

Emily thought for a moment, "How many groups of elves would we have to find? Five? Six?"

"Six I've found so far in that text," Will clarified.

"We portal jump to each one, speak to them, maybe have to persuade them. The antidotes would be...what? Other potions? Would they have them on hand or need to make them fresh?"

"I cannot say," Will sat up and hunched over, his elbows on his knees, his face much closer to Emily's, "And the problem is we do not know where these clans are. They keep their locations secret—even their own kind cannot find them if they do not want to be found."

"So we would be searching an entire region to hopefully find the right elves who may not even want to be found. If we end up finding them, they would need to either give us an antidote or we would need to convince them to make one. In the days we have left, we could possibly get half of them if we are lucky and the antidotes don't take too long to make?"

"If we go through with the party and the person is not there, we will have wasted all of that time. If they *are* there, then there is no way we can guarantee we can convince them to tell us where to find the antidote." There was a large *thump* as Will slammed his hand down on the chair's arm, causing the metal legs to shift under him against the stone floor.

Emily felt his frustration. She did not want to make the wrong move, especially given that she wasn't thinking with a clear head. He didn't want to make the wrong move because he had so much to lose—a friend, a fiancée, and she assumed a lofty position as the husband of the heir apparent. Her guilt in making the wrong choice would not be as strong as his. She placed her hand on his, "Let's go through with the party—that way nobody will think anything is up."

They sat in silence until the sound of furniture moving somewhere in the house cut through the quiet of the moment. Emily fiddled with the skirt of her dress, brushing off dust and pressing out creases. "I think Empath should be there."

Will nodded, staring past Emily to the wall behind her.

"Maybe Daughter of Brawn, too," she suggested, tucking her face into Will's line of sight.

Will blinked his eyes quickly, "Yes, yes," he cleared his throat with a gruff cough, "We should have all the allies we can get."

Emily smiled—Daughter of Brawn would get a few more stolen moments and Emily would not feel as alone. She imagined the entryway filled with people. Then remembered they would not be people, but demons and vampires, dwarves and elves, whatever else was outside of the walls of the two houses where she'd spent most her time. She could see a room of staring eyes, teeth, and sly smiles. She saw Belle and Wit tucked in a corner, Wit's lips whispering into Belle's ear as she laughed. Wit looked directly at Emily and took a sip of a dark red liquid. She heard someone yell, "Imposter!" and suddenly she was surrounded by pointing fingers. A spiral of flame began to engulf her.

"Emily?" This time it was Will who was creeping into Emily's line of sight.

The ghosts in Emily's mind turned to mist. Had Will gone through a similar thought process? Was he also terrified of what was ahead? Of course he was, but probably for different reasons. She took a breath and smiled as she let it out, "Is there anything else I can help with?" Her voice was butter, her mind was shattered glass.

"Are you ready for this?" Will asked with a furrowed brow, looking into her eyes. Both his hands were now on hers.

Will's face was *right there*. She felt a sudden urge to kiss him. If there was a moment to do so, this was it. All she would have to do is lean forward. Her lips parted slightly as she took in a deep breath. She pulled her hands away, "No," she whispered to herself.

"I thought as much," Will mirrored Emily, lying back into his chair once again.

Emily wanted to explain that she was not answering the question, but realized the response applied to her readiness, as well. "How many people—how many *individuals* will be there?"

Will let an amused burst of air escape his nostrils as he smirked, "As many as can come. The invitation is in the sky

116

tonight to all high-ranking...*individuals*...from the Dark Region, the Seas, and the Mountains. They would total in the hundreds if they were all present, but the sirens will not come—they can only go between land and sea a limited number of times before they lose their immortality. Not many dwarves will come this far from the mountains. The elves will send a few representatives, but not risk having all of their leaders in one place. Most of the crowd will be from the Dark Region, demons of all sorts and most of the vampires."

"Sorts of demons? There's more than one sort?" Emily asked.

"Most demons in Capital are fire demons, but some have a sort of link to other elements or to animals. Water demons live near the Seas or the river, earth demons are more comfortable near the Mountains. Within those factions, some can turn to animals from your world or have characteristics of them. Snakes," he gestured to himself, "for example."

Emily sat upright, "You can turn into a snake?"

Will shook his head, "No, but my father could. My mother's clan were exclusively fire demons, so I got the looks of my father and the skills of my mother. Though, my reactions can be quite quick in battle, which my father claims as his contribution."

"What about my dad?" Emily inquired.

"No animal link of which I am aware," Will shrugged, "but during the Grand Trial, he was seen using a multitude of powers—he does not know much of his lineage, but it must have many types of powerful demons. Unfortunately, not much of that ability seems to have transferred to your sister or yourself. That human blood seems to have muted many of those powers, as your sister's greatest power turned out to be her mind and social aptitude."

Emily wanted to tell him what she could do, but would he be upset that she and Empath went out in the middle of the day? Would he be mad that she went off to the lava fields? Would he

117

be jealous? Emily sighed, moving back to the topic at hand, "How dangerous is it to be half-human in a room full of dark creatures?"

"They all know your sister—and they all respect her," Will paused, "I suppose not all, but practically all. She has worked hard to prove she belongs here despite being human, though at times she still does not believe that to be the case," he trailed off momentarily, "But you will be with me. Empath and Daughter of Brawn will be around too, Wit has promised to watch over you, and you will be surrounded by people with their eyes on you as the demoness of the hour, so I doubt anyone would attempt to harm you at the party."

Emily felt a little bit of tension leave her shoulders, which reminded her to unclench her jaw. She had been rubbing the fingertips on her right hand together, and when she pulled them apart she could see an electric arc between her thumb and forefinger. She closed her hand quickly and looked back at Will, smiling as if nothing had happened, "You promise not to leave me?"

"I will try my best not to," his voice was not so assuring, "but as host I do have some responsibilities that may take me away. Every other moment will be yours, though."

The thought that Daughter of Brawn and Empath would be there, too, helped. She would seek one of them out should she need a companion. And Wit—Emily shook her head when he came to her mind, surprised that it had taken so long to remember he would be there to accompany her. Emily half-smiled and looked back up at Will, who had his nose in the potions book again. The longer she spent with Will, the closer she felt to him, but she was not allowed to feel that closeness. What she felt for Wit was intense and passionate. An M star and an O star—one reliable and slow-burning, one fast and hot. Emily chuckled to herself at the irony, Wit being compared to something that would kill him. How did she even remember the star classifications? *"Oh, be a fine guy, kiss me."* Either way, she would not be able to pursue either, since they would find a way to save her sister and she would never see either of them again.

"Excuse me?" Will was no longer reading—he was staring straight at Emily, his eyebrows well above their normal location.

Emily snapped out of her daydream, "What?"

"You asked me to kiss you," Will said with a slight chuckle.

Emily's breath caught—had she been thinking out loud? How much had she said? She was mortified, and realized she needed to explain. "Oh, be a fine guy, kiss me. It's a mnemonic: O-B-A-F-G-K-M—the order of stars from hottest and shortest-lived to least hot and longest burning." The words spilled out of her mouth quickly and awkwardly.

Will gave her a curious look, the tip of his tongue touching the corner of his mouth, just peeking out from his lips. He held that look for a moment, then went back to the book, no further questions.

Emily got up and put back the book she had been "reading." She went over the bookshelves and found titles written in a variety of languages—French, Arabic, Japanese, Russian, other languages she recognized but couldn't identify, and languages she couldn't even recognize. Everyone she had spoken to spoke English, but she had obviously only met a select subset of citizens. She picked out a book titled in English, *Elvish Clans of the Mountains*, to see if she could find information on Empath's clan. Unfortunately, there seemed to be dozens of major clans and no real way to tell which he was from without asking him.

She read about clans that specialized in transformations, in shapeshifting, in concealment, in potions, in power over the forests, in the creation of life. Very few had exact locations indicated, some offered nearby features like rivers or peaks, and others did not even offer a general location. They came from all over the world, but most clans that gave their origins were originally from Scandinavia and the British Isles.

Emily enjoyed just sitting and reading. She eventually laid down on her stomach on an animal skin rug, arching her back so she could rest on her elbows to continue reading. She remembered doing the same on her mom's old Moroccan rug behind the register, trying hard not to crease the books too much so they could still be sold as new. While one hand held the book open, the other pet the fur, feeling it slide under her fingertips. After she became uncomfortable holding up her torso, she turned onto her back, holding the book up on her chest, resting her head on her other forearm, growing much more comfortable by the moment.

Suddenly she awoke. Bright sunlight shot in through the cracks in the window coverings—either sunrise or sunset. Will was gone. She scrambled up to her feet and placed her book back on the shelf. Her shoes had fallen off, but she did not bother to put them back on, instead preferring to go about in her stocking feet.

She opened the library door slightly to find nobody in the foyer. Light was pouring in through the large windows—there were no covers in this room. Cautiously, she stepped out of the library to search for Will—or, at least, that would be her story if anybody caught her sneaking around the house. She wanted to get a better feel for the place, especially since she might need to take advantage of a hidden nook or space away from the crowd.

Emily found the ballroom easily—it was the room whose entrance was between the two large, curved staircases. On the main floor she also found a large dining room and two more large rooms, one seemed almost like a conference room and the other had musical instruments. She even found a hidden set of stairs that would take her downstairs into a dark, lightless basement, but she did not want to journey down there as she heard the sounds of pots and pans clinking about. This helped her confirm that the sun was setting and not rising, as the first meal of the night was being made.

As she was adventuring, she would sometimes allow her feet to skate across the marble floors. She was quite proud of herself when she was able to make it from the middle of a room to the other side in one go. She went up the stairs to the empty room in which they had practiced dancing, but did not dare to venture into any other rooms for fear she would wake someone up—she didn't know if there was anybody else staying here. Besides, night was falling and everyone would be awake soon. She made her way back downstairs when the front door clicked and screeched open. Emily stood there like a deer in headlights, only to find the other individual doing the same.

Wit's eyes were wide and his lips slightly parted as he met her gaze, "You...stayed for the day?"

Emily hurried down the last stairs. Her hair was a mess and she was slipping over her stocking feet, "No, no. I fell asleep in the library."

Wit pursed his lips, "The library is not upstairs."

Emily finally made it over to the doorway, nearly falling into his arms, "I know. I was just looking around before the staff woke up, I swear."

Wit held out his hands to help her balance herself. His hands were cold, but strong. He smiled at her, still not showing a full smile but obviously making an attempt to show pleasantness. He diverted his attention when the sound of footsteps came from the stairs.

Will was doing up his neck scarf—just a simple one, nothing fancy—as he was coming down the stairs, "Ah, you are awake. I was not sure if I should wake you or just leave you to sleep," he nodded at Wit, "And you, sir, are just the person I need to see. Thank you for coming so quickly. I have something to attend to first, though, will you wait?"

Wit nodded slowly, almost in a bow, "I will be in the music room with her Highness," he looked down at Emily and smiled, still holding onto her hand, "if she will join me."

Emily smiled sweetly and walked with him, hand-in-hand, to the music room. There were instruments piled into the room, making it seem messy and unorganized, but Emily attributed this to having extra instruments for the upcoming party. It was strange to see so many familiar instruments with no wooden parts to them—pianos, violins, and basses all made from metal. She wondered if they all sounded the same, so she went and sat at the piano, hitting a single key. The short, low note filled the room and bounced back to her—it resonated within the metal quite well.

"They're enchanted," Wit noted, sitting down beside her, resting his fingers lightly on the keys, "They sound like the traditional instruments, but no wood." He began to play a low, dramatic song. "Out of consideration for the vampires, there is no wood in this region. No green vegetation. No mirrors. But magic allows us to make do without such frivolous things." He was able to talk over his playing effortlessly.

Emily stared at him, his hands gliding over the keys, his eyes barely glancing down at them, "How long have you been playing the piano?"

"I've played the piano since it was created," he continued playing the song, changing it into a minor key, giving it a slightly threatening mood, "but played harpsichord in my youth. I can play any of those," he nodded his head in the direction of the great mess of instruments, "It's one of the benefits of living so long," he abruptly ended his playing, playing the last chord rather forcefully, "you have time to learn anything you'd like."

Emily looked toward the door, ensuring they were still alone, "I hope you don't think I was doing anything...improper during the day."

"It did enter my mind that you might feel certain ways after spending so much time with Will," Wit rose and turned toward a still-shuttered window, opening it to let the night air in, "It would not have surprised me if you had acted on those feelings."

Emily followed him to the window, holding his arm tightly as she hugged him from the side. Her body heat escaped into him, "I do not have those feelings for my sister's fiancé. I am quite captivated by someone else." In the moment, her words were the truth.

Emily heard someone clear their throat behind them. Emily's arm shot down as she turned around. It was Will, who looked sternly at them, "Wit, I can see you now." He turned away from the door without acknowledging Emily.

The slight from Will stung. She started as if to go after him, but Wit grabbed her hand and gently pulled her back, reassuring her, "He will be fine. He is offended if he is not at the forefront of every maiden's mind."

Wit turned Emily's face to look at him and any concern melted away. She trusted Wit completely; something in his eyes took away any doubts or fears. Emily knew the ball would be fine so long as Wit was around.

"I will come for you when I am done here, Highness," Wit kissed Emily's hand and left.

Emily turned back to the piano. She sat down, resting her fingers on the keys. She'd taken piano lessons when she was younger from the owner of the music shop next door but hadn't touched a piano in years. She tucked most of her fingers back into her hand, leaving only her index fingers on the keys. She quickly tapped out "Chopsticks" and pulled her hands away, letting the last note resonate in the room. She smiled to herself and turned around to find the footman standing, confused, in the doorway. Emily kept a neutral face and said, "I see you are in need of this room. I will see myself out."

Chapter Eleven

Emily stood alone in the courtyard just outside of Will's house, staring at her father's carriage. The driver was nowhere to be seen. Of course, she did not expect him to sit there waiting for her the entire day, but how was she supposed to get back to the palace? She spun in circles, trying to eye him, hoping he would just happen to come back at that moment. None of Will's staff had come outside with her.

"Driver?" she tried.

Summoned out of thin air, the driver was seated on the front of the coach, tipping his hat to Emily. She curtsied, realizing on her way back up she should probably learn how to curtsy properly before the ball. How was it just two nights away now?

She entered the carriage and they started moving. Emily opened the window and tucked her head out, calling to the driver, "Might we go to the lava fields tonight?"

"Of course, Highness," the driver whipped the reins attached to nothingness in front of him. Did they actually serve a purpose or were they just for show?

Before she had left, Emily retrieved her shoes from the library. While she was in there, she picked out another book off of the shelf—*The Art of Fire* by Flame of Foothill, apparently an authority on the topic. She untucked it from the folds of her skirt and began reading to pass the time. Conveniently, this book was just what she needed before she went to practice her magic. It had diagrams, breathing techniques, and even incantations to better control the use of fire magic. Thankfully, the incantations included phonetic spelling, as they were in yet another language Emily did not know. She whispered the words under her breath to practice the feel of them in her mouth. Some were clunky, but others more fluid.

She was about five chapters into the book when they came to a stop where the road came closest to the lava field. Emily stepped out and, without looking at the driver, told him, "I will call when I am ready. Thank you." She heard a *whip* and turned to find him gone once more while the carriage remained on the side of the road.

Emily stepped onto the bed of black rock that stretched into the darkness. The sulfuric smell carried on the wind as it whipped the stray pieces of hair into her face. She walked until she could no longer see the road, then walked further still to ensure she would have privacy. The moonlight shone on the smooth igneous rock below her, giving it a silver sheen.

She opened the book once more, to the third chapter. Emily snapped the fingers of her free hand and it ignited, giving her more light to read by. She whispered the words she found and pulled her hand down—the flame stayed exactly where it was, not entering the space where her fingers had been. Emily walked around it, admiring the floating, negative-space fire statue. She circled her hand around the flame and it extinguished immediately.

She looked back in the book to find another phrase she had encountered in her reading. She read it three times before gently tossing the book down a few feet away. She stood tall, squared her shoulders, and took a deep breath. She held her hands above her head and whispered another incantation, then threw her arms down. A fire encased her, starting from her head all the way down to the ground as her hands passed by. She once again whispered the incantation that held fire in its place, then stepped out of the fire. Her effigy remained in flame. Fire caressed her image's cheeks, hair, shoulders, and dress.

Emily admired the figure before her. She hadn't seen herself in a week—she looked changed, stronger somehow. It felt a little narcissistic to be staring at herself for so long like this, but for a moment she was transfixed. This frozen moment of a half-demoness performing a spell was inspiring. She wanted to be this confident woman all of the time. She wanted to carry this image with her to remind her of this time in her life, especially when she went back to her world—back to being powerless and grey.

A wind whipped her hair, bringing her back to the present. She left the image where it was while she went to look through the book again. After sitting on the fields for so long, the cover was hot; much longer sitting on the rock and it might have caught fire. She sat in the firelight and searched for another technique she wanted to try. When she found it, she waved away the fiery Emily and it vanished as quickly as it had ignited.

Emily crossed her legs and began breathing slowly, feeling her chest rise and fall. She was supposed to be taking deeper breaths, filling her lungs, but it was not entirely possible while seated and in this dress. She held her hands to her sides, her palms flat and facing upward. She lifted them slowly, feeling a weight in her hands and exertion in her arms. The ground beneath her cracked and quaked. A sudden snap made the piece of land she was seated on jolt suddenly upward. She kept her focus but smiled, knowing it was working. She raised her hands higher and she was lifted. She was not sure how high she was, since she kept her eyes shut, but once she was content, she finally opened her eyes and set down her hands. She laid on her belly and peered down off the edge, seeing she was at least twenty feet above the fields, on a solid cap atop a podium of molten rock. The ground beneath her glowed from the fire she pulled from the earth.

She saw something far below which made her heart sink— the book. She had practiced going up, but never thought to check how to get down. She considered climbing down but she was not about to stick her hand in lava. She could test her heat tolerance later when someone was around to heal her. She considered jumping; demons have unnatural strength, right? Should she risk breaking a leg while alone in the middle of nowhere?

After some consideration, she stood and held her left hand out over the edge, palm up and flat, and whispered the incantation once more. She pulled up another column, a smaller circle, to about two feet below her. She stepped onto it and pulled yet another, creating descending stairs. She made each one slightly to the left of the last so when she reached the ground once more, the eleven columns created a cascading spiral. The columns cooled when she stepped off, so they became igneous pillars of rock. She found some mild amusement in that she created some Art of Fire.

Emily picked up the book, looked back approvingly at her work, and headed to the road. On the way, she held her left hand out, palm down with her fingers trailing as if to trace lines in the air. Below her hand, four streaks of fire appeared, reaching out of the rock. She used her fingers to doodle lines and designs. At one point, she wrote her name—*Emily*—then washed it away with a wave of lava.

When she reached the road, she looked back at the fields one more time, breathing in the minerals rising up from the rock. The hot air was cut by a cool breeze from inland that pushed at her back, causing her to stumble towards the dark abyss. She considered going back out but instead called for the driver as she held the book to her breast. He appeared instantly, notifying her of an individual waiting for her at the palace.

On the drive home she continued reading, taking mental note of the pages she would like to revisit. She resisted every urge to dog-ear the book, as she hadn't even received permission to borrow it. She would have to sneak it back into Will's house some other time.

They arrived at the palace and as she walked to the front door, Emily threw her hands to her sides and the doors opened with fire licking the handles before it extinguished. Inside the doorway she saw Wit, clearly amused by her trick. When she stepped inside, the doors shut behind her. She and Wit did not move into the main hall but stayed tucked away in the entryway.

Wit took the book from her hands, "Some light reading?" He held the book up in front of his face but let the top edge of it rest on his nose. He inhaled, smelling the cover. He closed his eyes, apparently appreciating the smell, then smirked once again, "Some light *practice*? Someone has been to the lava fields again."

Emily took the book back from him, "Just a detour on the way home."

"And what did her Highness learn today?" Wit leaned his body closer to Emily's.

Emily tucked back, looking into the main hall, checking to see if anyone was around. When she saw nobody, she went back to Wit, bringing her body even closer to his, "A little of this," she looked up into his eyes, "a little of that."

Wit smiled knowingly, his teeth showing. Emily drew in a short breath and Wit quickly backed away. She reached out to grab him by the hip, "Don't. I'm not afraid," she pulled him back to the closeness they had before, "I was just happy you actually smiled."

Wit rested his hand against the wall over Emily's shoulder, bringing his face down to meet hers, "You are supposed to be afraid," he said playfully with a large grin, "Do they not tell tales of vampires anymore?"

Emily looked him in the eyes. She could get lost in them if she let herself, "They're just stories."

Wit slowly brought his face closer to Emily. Emily closed her eyes, waiting for their lips to meet, but she heard a *clunk* beside her as someone unlatched the door from the outside. She quickly ducked under Wit's arm, scurried out into the main room, and looked up at the walkways of the second and third floors, as if she had been doing so for some time.

A member of the house staff stopped in the doorway, "I am sorry, your Highness, I was under the impression nobody was home. I will bring this shipment in through the back doorway." He tucked back out the door and shut it behind him.

Emily turned back to Wit, "That was close."

He walked up to her, graceful as always, and took her hand. He lightly kissed her fingers and tugged her arm to pull her close. He whispered in her ear, "In my opinion, Highness, it was not close enough."

Shivers were sent down Emily's spine. She pushed him away lightly, "Someone will hear you," she said coyly as she looked around, checking that they were still alone, "you should go before we get in trouble."

"Whatever you wish, your Highness," Wit took her hand and brought it up as if to kiss it once more, but paused, "but before I leave, I must know if you've chosen a dress for the ball."

Emily's eyes widened. How was she supposed to get a dress? Did it need to be something extravagant? Would she even be able to move in it? Were the hips going to be five feet wide? How "18th Century" did the traditionalists like it? Emily squeaked out a simple, "No."

Wit smiled and squeezed her hand, "Fret not. I will have a dressmaker over tomorrow—one that has not worked with your sister yet, so you will not have to convince her of who you are, but still one of great reputation."

Emily contorted her face and squeezed out one last, foolish question, "Powdered wigs?"

Wit shook his head, "Those days are long over, thankfully."

Emily relaxed. "Thankfully," she repeated.

Wit kissed her hand and left, but not without looking back at her and smiling a laughing smile. Emily wanted to call him back or run after him but held her ground since she heard doors opening and closing on the upper landings. After pausing a moment to admire her mother's portrait, she went back to her sister's room. As she turned to close the door, Daughter of Brawn appeared in the doorway.

"He sure is a rare specimen," she noted, whispering, as she smiled up at Emily, "I doubt many vampires would be able to be that close to a human without losing their composure."

Emily signaled her friend into the room and shut the door behind her, leaning on it with all her weight, "You were watching?"

"Was I not supposed to?" she asked as she traced her finger along the door frame as Emily got out of her way, "You were in the main room—anyone could have seen you."

"I didn't see anyone around," Emily retorted, "most individuals are not as sneaky as you are."

Daughter of Brawn beamed, "I thank your Highness for the compliment."

"I guess he is something special," Emily mused, "I've never met anyone like him."

"You have not met anyone like any of us before," the small demoness pointed out, "and you surely have never met a vampire before."

Emily's pleasant demeanor changed, "You aren't about to lecture me about this again, are you?"

"No," Daughter of Brawn's eyes widened, radiating their lavender hue, "Of course not, Highness. I was simply stating this is all new to you and likely exciting. It must be difficult to get your bearings."

Emily relaxed as she sat down on the bed, "I suppose everyone is a lot more gentle than I expected them to be. Dark creatures left behind a bit of a legacy back home—not a good one."

"Well, you are far nicer than I expected," Daughter of Brawn shrugged, "Your sister was born here, so of course she is kind, but we were not sure what to expect from someone raised by a human in the human world."

"I can't speak for the people hundreds of years ago, but I don't think we're too bad now," Emily reconsidered, "Not sure how they would react if they were not the most powerful creatures in the world, though. People get scared pretty easily when they don't feel in control."

"And do you feel in control?" The sharp purple eyes flashed.

Emily paused to consider this, then nodded slowly with a slight furrow to her brow, "I think I'm starting to."

"Grand," Daughter of Brawn smiled and bounded over to the closet, "Because we need to try on some dresses so you can tell the dressmaker what you would like tomorrow. Then we can discuss," she looked back at Emily and said in her best French accent, "accoutrements."

Emily never enjoyed shopping, but that was because she never could afford much. To get to try on so many dresses, then tell someone the exact style and color and fabric she would like seemed like a dream. She never got dolled up or went out, so this was a new adventure, and Daughter of Brawn seemed more than happy to help.

They pulled out a dress of each style and laid them on the bed—about five were considered to be appropriate for a ball of this magnitude. They laughed and talked about the ball while

Daughter of Brawn helped Emily in and out of each dress. Daughter of Brawn had never attended one herself, but she had heard about many and had the general idea of what would happen. Most balls started at twilight. Nobody would want to risk the event running long and going into the daytime, trapping the more light-sensitive individuals.

"You would likely go just after you break your fast," Daughter of Brawn noted.

"We," Emily said, throwing down yet another stiff, suffocating dress, "You and Empath are coming too."

Daughter of Brawn lit up, then quickly became quiet and dropped her head, "I cannot. It would not be proper for me to be in the room with those guests."

"You can, as an ambassador from the Mountains my sister met on her latest travels. Not a noble, but a daughter of a dwarf we've been in dealings with," Emily picked up one of the dresses and thrust it at Daughter of Brawn, "Now try this on, Cinderella."

Daughter of Brawn stood there with the dress in her arms, staring in disbelief while Emily picked up a fourth dress. The black dress had buttons all down the back and no coat—it seemed much less restrictive. Emily undid the buttons and pulled up over her waist. She pulled on the sleeves and smoothed the area over her torso. Now that Daughter of Brawn was occupied in putting on a dress for herself, Emily managed the buttons herself by pantomiming in front of her. She had to keep restarting, as she kept misaligning the buttons without realizing until she reached the top.

Daughter of Brawn noticed this by the fourth attempt and went over to help, "Allow me, your Highness. Buttons are not as simple as knots and bows." She pushed Emily's hair out of the way and worked her way up the dozens of buttons. When it was on, Emily turned around and returned the favor for the laces on the back of Daughter of Brawn's dress.

They eyed each other for a moment, then smiled, both agreeing that their respective dress was perfect.

Daughter of Brawn noted first, "Yours is a more modern fashion, but still appropriate for the ball. A bold choice, but you can be a bold individual when it suits you. The color will need to be different, and I can anticipate there may be other textiles you can choose from—your sister loves the simplicity of wool, but it may be more comfortable in another material."

Emily twirled slightly. The skirt had volume, but not nearly as much as other dresses she had worn since she arrived. The material hugged her torso, but she admitted to needing some sort of shapewear to help support her breasts, as the cut along the top showed a good part of her chest. The dressmaker would have input, too, so she decided to use this as only a starting point and let the expert weigh in when it was time.

Daughter of Brawn was in a more traditional style. It was very large on her, but she looked extravagant in the black dress with purple frills. She looked like she belonged in an 18th century ball, which would help her fit in with the more traditional types that would attend. Emily asked, "Will you be able to move comfortably in that skirt?" It was a wider shape with cushions holding it up over her hips. Emily hated trying it on for that reason.

"Yes, I believe so," Daughter of Brawn smiled, patting her huge hips, "It's not too much larger than my normal skirts. Additionally," she placed her hands in slits in the sides of the dress that aligned with slits in the cushions, "It has pockets."

"Do you think you can do the alterations yourself?" Emily asked.

Daughter of Brawn nodded, "Easily. I had been training as a ladies' maid under the last one who served your sister, but when she left for her trial nobody was chosen to replace her—your sister either did things herself or had her Lady-in-waiting help."

Emily thought about the beautiful woman who had kissed her, "What happened to Belle? Did she leave?"

Daughter of Brawn shrugged, "I do not believe anybody knows. They were all focused on what was happening in here."

Emily looked at Daughter of Brawn, concerned, "Do they all know?"

Daughter of Brawn smiled back, "No, we explained it away as being a lovers' quarrel," She turned to get her regular clothes while she quoted, "*Heaven has no rage like love to hatred turned, nor hell a fury like a woman scorned.*"

As the sun began to rise, they agreed that Daughter of Brawn would act as ladies' maid while the dressmaker was present, so she could help her with the specific language she would need to get the dress she wanted and keep her from accidentally revealing too much.

Daughter of Brawn left with the new dress in her arms, leaving Emily to some much-needed rest.

Chapter Twelve

The next night, Emily ate her first meal with her father, continuing their conversation from a few nights before. They talked about what it was like to grow up in the human world and how Champion came to power in this world.

The battle royale was held in Capital's city center, so young Dagger had the advantage of knowing the back alleys and side streets he could sneak through. All civilians were relocated, and everything and anything in-bounds was able to be used for survival or battle.

Dagger's strategy was to lie low until the others killed off or forced the surrender of the majority. Not many of them came after him, as they did not expect him to be a major threat.

When he finally did enter the combat on the third night, he was relentless—taking out some of the top competitors within his first hour. He took out the crowd favorite, a vampire, by melting the metal roof he was sheltering under in the daytime.

Emily and Champion continued to talk, even after their meal had been cleared and the leftovers went cold. It seemed the only topic that was not mentioned was Emily being there—as if her father wanted to be sure she knew he did not approve of her presence in this world. There was no mention of the plans or the ball, nothing about Will. He did not mention her sister explicitly, just in relation to his own life in the region. Even recognizing this, Emily could have sat there to talk for hours, but a footman came in to interrupt.

"Your Highness," he said with a slight bow, "The dressmaker has arrived. Shall I have her set up in the East Room?"

Emily frowned, "I find that room rather drafty, make up the Blue Room if it is available."

The footman left with a nod.

The woman who had set up her materials in the Blue Room had a mousey face. As she continued observing her, Emily noticed that many of her features were mouse-like. She had long, slender fingers that moved quickly. She bit thread with her sharp teeth to cut it. Emily realized it was not a coincidence when she found the woman had two circular, furry ears on top of her head. Emily coughed lightly and the ear closest to her twitched.

"Your Highness," she said in a melodious voice much deeper in pitch than Emily had expected as she curtsied dramatically to the floor.

Daughter of Brawn stepped in behind Emily, carrying the black dress, "Your Highness, may I present Craft." She brought the dress to Craft's workstation and set it down, "Her Highness would like her dress in a more modern style like this."

Craft thumbed the material and lifted the sleeve, "That can be done, but not wool," she directed her comments to Daughter of Brawn, "Wool is too warm for a demon in a crowded room. The heat will stifle her. Might I suggest silk?"

Daughter of Brawn walked back to Emily's side, "You would have to ask her Highness."

Emily walked over to the bolts of fabric the woman had laid out, a mosaic of rich colors and textures. She was drawn to a red one that seemed to shine in the torchlight and lightly touched her hand to it. It was so soft to the touch compared to everything else she had worn. "Perhaps like this one?"

Craft smiled, "Wit said you might be drawn to red." She unrolled some of the indicated fabric and held it out for Emily to appraise. Where the fabric was exposed to light, it was a bright blood red, but the parts in the shadows appeared to have a more sultry hue—a deep, mysterious shade.

Emily ran her hand over it and watched the material as it bent and moved. The motion of it would be perfect for the dress, especially if she were to be dancing in it. Dancing. She needed to practice the dances again. There was less than 24 hours before she would be needing to dance in front of a room full of people.

Craft brought her face into Emily's line of sight to break her train of thought, "Is... this a good fabric for you, your Highness?"

Emily nodded quickly, "Yes, yes," she smiled, "I am terribly sorry, just imagining what it would look like as a dress."

Craft smiled back, "No need to imagine, we will create it now. Please undress."

Daughter of Brawn helped Emily out of the dress she was wearing. She kept on her stay, but Craft pulled out a different stay and held it to Daughter of Brawn, "Put her in this. It will suit this kind of dress better than what she has now. And she will not need her shift."

Emily turned to give Daughter of Brawn a wide-eyed look of horror—she was *not* about to strip naked in front of this stranger. Daughter of Brawn left the room for a moment and came back carrying a large privacy screen. The metal frame was bulky and looked heavy, but she carried it with ease. She set it up and pulled Emily behind it. She stuck her head out from the side and asked, "Is there something for her to wear under this?"

The dressmaker threw a small piece of cloth, just small enough to fit under the stay. Daughter of Brawn looked back, confused, but Craft simply stated, "It will make the stay comfortable, cover important areas, and still allow me to design as I wish." She waved her hand as if to shoo Daughter of Brawn away.

When the stay was on, Emily's eyes popped—and they were not the only feature of hers that appeared larger. She could hardly see her toes past her bosom. She turned to Daughter of Brawn while still hidden behind the screen and mouthed, "Is this enchanted?" while pointing at her chest.

"No," came a voice from the other side of the screen, "Just a good design, your Highness." Craft walked behind the screen to see how the stay fit. It felt more like a corset—Emily brought her hands down her sides and noticed an hourglass figure that had not been there before. Surprisingly, it also allowed a bit more breathing room than her sister's other wardrobe staples. Craft asked, "Is this to your liking?"

"Very much so," Emily could only think about Wit and what his reaction might be. She hoped he would only have eyes for her that evening.

Craft went back out to a metal platform and indicated she wanted Emily to stand on it. She took some of the fabric and draped it over her hips, creating the skirt. Emily hadn't noticed that Craft had heavily pierced ears until she started pulling out pins from the thin cartilage and pinning the skirt to the corset. As she was pinning, the remaining cloth was unrolling itself and hovering over where Craft would need it next.

It took less time than Emily expected to get the basic shape of the dress. At one point, Craft asked, "Is this what you were thinking, your Highness?" Emily looked down to see she was essentially in a copy of the original dress—just in the new fabric. The fine details were not finished, of course, but the basic form was identical.

"It is a nice dress," Emily noted with a somewhat disappointed tone, "and I love the fabric, but I feel it should be," she paused, trying to find the right word, but gave up when she realized her silence had been too long, "...more...for the occasion."

Craft nodded, "I can add details to the bottom to make it more elegant. Perhaps some detail on the sleeve, as well? The buttons up the back will add a level of intricacy, as well."

Emily was more keen on the dress with that suggestion, but her mind wandered back to Wit, "Would it be possible to make it more…" Again, she was at a loss for words, but gestured at her chest until she came up with a word at last, "alluring?"

"A special treat for your fiancé?" Craft pulled at the top of the dress, pulling the sleeves down over her shoulders, and put her finger to her mouth in thought. She winked at Emily, "Or perhaps showing the other gentlemen what they can no longer attain?"

Emily let a slight smile sneak onto her lips, "Something like that." As she reached down to toy with the skirt, she turned to look at Daughter of Brawn, whose absentminded frown gave the impression she did not approve. Emily was not sure if it was about the dress or about her reaction to Craft's remark but did not want to ask in front of the dressmaker.

"I believe I can make those adjustments," Craft stepped back and gave the dress a once-over, "If you can just step out of the dress, I can put it together and have it ready by sunset."

Emily was surprised by how quickly the appointment went. She doubted whether the dress could actually be done in less than a day, but she had no other choice but to trust the dressmaker. She stepped off the platform and slid the fabric off her body. She changed out of the shapewear and back into her dress behind the screen.

Craft bundled up the dress in her arms while her bolts of fabric and other tools all put themselves into the platform Emily had been standing on, which had turned itself over to become a sort of crate. The fabric rolls seemed to each wait its turn to organize itself into the box along with the others. By the end, there was a tightly-packed crate that hovered behind Craft and followed her out of the room.

Emily went to sit on the neatly-made bed in the room, but just as she was lowering herself Empath knocked on the open door, "I sense this is not the best time, but it seems as if we are running out of opportunities—should we practice the dance?"

Emily groaned as she collapsed to the bed and draped her arm over her eyes, "Do I have to?"

Empath struggled to respond, "I suppose… I suppose your Highness may not need…?"

Emily sat back up on the bed again, "Yes. Yes, I have to. We all know I need it. You can say it." She was not used to people trying not to offend her. She needed them to work on their balance of propriety and honesty, "Let's do it." Emily got to her feet and held her hand out for Empath to take. Daughter of Brawn took a seat on the bed and held the tall metal bedpost, leaning her head against it. She smiled at the two dancers.

Emily had a hard time remembering the sequence of steps. She was kicking herself for not setting aside more time to perfect it. All eyes would be on her the next night and she would be absolutely lost. Emily fumbled more as her mind wandered to images of whispering demons and monsters, elegantly dressed and turning their noses up at her.

Empath continued to dance, looking forward but still speaking to Emily, "It will be fine. The ladies will be too distracted, trying to catch the eye of some powerful official or suitor. The gentlemen will watch, but they will not be concerned with your steps. Even so, you do not need to impress them. Being engaged, your sister would never feel pressure to impress anyone ever again."

Emily nodded, jostling the negative images from her mind. She thought about the fiery image of her—a confident young woman who finally saw herself as such. The steps came easier and she could fudge the ones she could not remember well enough. She relaxed even further in realizing that Will would be there to dance with her. She was beginning to trust him more now that she understood how much emotional strain he must have been experiencing. He was investing heavily in Emily's success and needed her to be fully committed to the plan.

Emily was committed. She would get to go home after this.

She would *have* to go home after this.

Little Orphan Emily. Emily who was barely scraping by. Emily who wanted more out of life. Emily who had nobody to love her—romantically, lustfully, platonically, or paternally. Emily who was saving pennies so she could one day run away and start over somewhere else. She did not realize she had stopped dancing and Empath had stopped humming until Empath's voice cut the silence.

"We will miss you, as well," Empath pulled Emily in for a hug. His long, slender arms wrapped around her and filled her with warmth. Another set of arms could be felt in the embrace as Daughter of Brawn joined in. They all paused there for a moment as Emily's eyes welled with tears. She was determined to not let any fall. She had things to do. Empath, of course, knew exactly the right moment to break his hold. His hand went back out for Emily to take as they began the dance again from the top.

After a few more hours, Emily was prepared but worn out. She sat on the bed next to Daughter of Brawn and leaned against the other bedpost, "Thanks," she said to Empath, "I feel like there are more important things you could be doing instead of helping me learn a dance."

"Your father has put me completely at your disposal until you go," Empath reassured, "Besides, the most important affair in this region is the safety of our princess," he paused, waiting to catch Emily's eye, "of both of our princesses."

Emily did not need anybody to tell her the sun would be up soon—her energy level told her enough. When she laid down in her sister's bed, she thought she would be able to sleep right away, but she was kept up with thoughts of all the ways the next night could go wrong. She had been reassured again and again, but could not get over the impending sense of doom. When she finally got to sleep, she tossed and turned. She could not remember exactly what her dreams were about, but based on her anxiety upon waking up, they were not pleasant.

Chapter Thirteen

Emily's mouth gaped at the completed dress. The red silk was just as luscious, but embroidered details graced the bottom of the dress and climbed up the skirt, swirling in and out of recognizable patterns. The sleeves were barely there, just a ghost of the detailing from the bottom with no fabric to adhere to—a lace that would delicately hold her upper arm. She was speechless. All she could do was admire it and graze it with her fingertips.

How badly Emily wanted a mirror the moment the last button went on. She wanted to look in front of her and see how beautiful the dress was. She could feel it—that confidence that comes with the perfect outfit. She could feel her waist curving in, just enough to give the hourglass figure she had chased so long. She ran her hands down to the skirt, where her hips were given slight emphasis by the pleating of the fabric that quickly smoothed out to a full, but not exaggerated, shape. Her collarbone was completely visible, as the sleeves did not cover the shoulders, but started in line with the top of the bodice, which went straight across her chest, just barely letting the tops of her breasts peek out. And the color—that blood-red that was both romantic and full of lust—was exactly the color that came to mind when Emily was asked what her favorite color was.

"What do you think?" Emily asked as she gave a spin, holding one side of the skirt and tossing it dramatically as she came to a stop.

"It is lovely," Daughter of Brawn said hesitantly, "but it does draw a great deal of attention to your neck."

Emily's hands went to her neck and slid down over her shoulders, "Emphasize your best features, I suppose." Her hands slid over her collarbone, upon which she hooked her fingers and let her arms rest, "Do you think it is too much? Wit has restrained himself so far, I don't think he'd try anything."

"Wit will not be the only vampire in attendance," Daughter of Brawn noted, "but I suppose if he is going to help protect you, we should not have anything to fear." She smiled at Emily, having put herself more at ease, "It is truly an astounding dress."

Emily smiled excitedly and let out a small squeal, "Is yours ready? Can I see it?"

Daughter of Brawn shook her head, "Almost. I must go finish it, if you can spare me."

Emily shooed her away, "Yes! Go! Get all dolled up!"

Daughter of Brawn paused in the door, "Your hair?"

Emily reached for her hair—it was down, but she could not even tell what state it was in. She checked the color, it was brown, as it needed to be for the evening. "Would it be acceptable to wear it down? Maybe use it to cover the shoulders if they're getting too much attention?"

Daughter of Brawn grabbed a brush, "If you would please sit, I have an idea."

Emily sat in the metal chair in front of the open window. The cool evening air hit Emily's neck whenever her hair was lifted, sending goosebumps across her skin. The sensation reminded her of an icy touch. She imagined fingers caressing the back of her neck. *Why not?* she thought, *I am only here for a short*

144

time, why not make the most of it? She would do it—just for the hell of it, she would let something happen. Of course, she would still be working to save her sister, but she would also do this one thing for herself.

When Daughter of Brawn was finished, the brown hair shone in the torchlight. She felt the top of her head and found two small braids coming from the front to be tied in the back, then flow down with the rest of her hair.

"Would you like to see?" Daughter of Brawn asked.

Emily stared at her, wide-eyed, "You've been keeping a mirror from me?"

"No," Daughter of Brawn made her way over to a window and held her hand to it. The area outside the window darkened with a black smoke, creating a reflection in the glass, "But we have ways to work around such rules."

Emily was once again struck by the power of her own image. The reflection was not sharp, but the softness of her features added to the allure. The only thing that would make it better was if she looked like herself—not her sister. She missed seeing her blonde hair. She missed her unmarked arm. The difference was subtle, but enough to realize nobody would truly see *her* today.

As her left hand absentmindedly grazed her right arm, Emily's attention came back to Daughter of Brawn, "What are you still doing here? Go get ready!"

The moment Daughter of Brawn took her hand from the window, the dark cloud disappeared, taking Emily's reflection with it. She scurried out of the room excitedly, turning around to whisper a "Good luck!" to Emily just before she disappeared.

Emily made her way downstairs. She kept her eyes forward but could not help noticing admiring glances from the house staff. She heard two maids whispering to each other but could tell it was not malicious. Champion was standing at the foot of the stairs, reaching up a hand to help Emily down the last few steps. He kissed her hand when she came to a stop.

145

"I am so very proud of you," he said, "You will be the most beautiful woman in the room." He pulled her in and wrapped his arms around her. She sank into his embrace and pressed her face into his chest. Champion whispered, "Please be safe. I cannot bear the thought of losing both of you."

Emily realized this might be the last time she saw her father and squeezed him even harder. Through light tears, she whispered, "Mom always told me that you loved us very much. I love you, too."

Champion said nothing but kept his hold of her. Emily could feel his chest shudder while he breathed. He leaned in and kissed the top of her head, pausing there for a few moments before finally letting go. When Emily turned her head up to look at his face, his eyes were red and swollen.

Emily bit her lips together to halt her own sobs as she made her way to the carriage waiting outside.

When she arrived at Will's house, there was a line of carriages waiting to drop off their passengers. While many had nothing pulling them, like her own, a handful were pulled by an assortment of creatures. One that was leaving as she entered the gated area had beautiful black horses with something slightly off about them. Emily's eyes widened as she whispered under her breath, "Those are freaking unicorns." She just had a chance to see white horns glisten in the moonlight as they passed.

The carriage directly in front of Emily's was pulled by two small, black dragons. They were biting at each other while their passenger stepped out, one spitting fire into the other's face. The woman had sleek, jet black hair that was pulled up into an intricate bun, pinned by gold clips dripping in red gems. They added a beautiful accent to the flowing, red robes that covered her black skirt, both of which had gold patterns printed on them. The woman turned to Emily, smirking with her deep red lips. She was not a young woman, but she was absolutely beautiful.

Emily noticed her fingertips had gripped the windowsill and her entire body was almost pressed against the pane in trying to get a closer look. She pulled away as quickly as she could when she noticed the woman looking at her. She needed to be cool about all of this—it is all completely normal for her sister. Nothing should shock her.

When it was her turn to go, Empath was there to open the door. His smile warmed her heart and gave her renewed confidence. She took his hand for stability as she descended the two steps to the gravel beneath. Loud conversations and music floated from the open door before her. The house looked alive with a warm glow coming from every window.

Bodies filled the foyer—rich colors swirled and slid across the room as heat spilled into the outside air. Emily readied herself and pulled her shoulders back, a slight breeze of fresh air whipping her hair to the side. She stepped into the room and saw one, two sets of eyes on her. More heads turned and the music stopped playing. Suddenly, the entire room dropped and rose as women curtsied and men bowed. Emily gave a slight nod of acknowledgement and the music began again. Some went back to doing what they had been doing—talking and drinking, but a few eyes lingered on her. Emily noted the faces, none of which betrayed any ill intentions, while Empath came in the door behind her. "Anything yet?" Emily asked over her shoulder.

"No," Empath said through nearly-closed lips, "But your attire is making quite the impression."

Emily smirked and made eye contact with some of the faces still looking at her. Some looked away quickly, some nodded, but one shot back with a look of approval in his eyes and a malicious smile on his lips. Emily stared back until Wit finally smiled enough to show his teeth. Feeling victorious, Emily walked into the main hall to find her pretend fiancé.

Her search did not take long. Will always looked put-together, but today he was downright polished. He wore a deep blue suit, still keeping with the traditional short breeches and long coat, over a gold silk vest. The gold detailing on the coat was as intricate as Emily's skirt—this had clearly been made for special occasions such as this. He did not take his eyes off of her the entire time she was approaching him. The sea of people seemed to part for them. When she finally met him, he took her hand, bowed as he kissed it, then came close for the kiss on her cheek, "It's me. You are absolutely breathtaking." His whispered breath on her skin in combination with the words from his lips made her blush slightly as she looked down toward the floor. "Shall I make the announcement?"

Emily raised her eyes, bit her lip, and nodded. It was time. Will led her to the platform on which the band was playing. He hopped onto it spryly, then helped Emily with the large step up. When the party noticed their presence on the stage, the room once again began to fall silent. Will put his hand on the side of his neck and spoke. His voice boomed as if it were being amplified, "Ladies and Gentlemen of darkness. Esteemed guests from regions beyond the mist. Thank you for journeying here tonight to celebrate with me," he looked over to Emily and smiled so sweetly Emily's heart would have melted had she felt it were genuine, "to celebrate with *us*. The reason I have called you to join me is that I have been promised the hand of Daughter of Champion upon her naming."

Emily's eyes scanned the crowd of guests applauding politely. Different hues of skin, widely varying heights, and a variety of cultural dress were all represented. She again saw the woman who arrived with the dragons—she wore a smug expression as she looked up at Will. Emily looked to Will, then back at the woman. As she tried to piece together their relationship, she caught sight of Empath, whose attention was drawn to the side of the room, a concerned look on his face.

Will continued, "It is my honor to ask the princess to join me in opening the ball with a dance from her mother's culture, as learned from texts her father brought with him from the human world." He held his hand out to Emily, who took it and looked up at Will once more. He was in his element tonight. His smile *was* genuine. He was finding some way, in all of this madness, to enjoy himself.

The doors to the ballroom opened and the candles flickered to life with a wave of Will's hand. He swept his hand around him, guiding Emily into position. The band began the three-quarter time song and Will led the steps. The dance was natural to them now. Emily got butterflies realizing how well things were going.

"You really know how to throw a party, huh?" Emily asked quietly so as to not be heard by onlookers over the volume of the music. The guests, swarmed in a wide circle around them, were a blur to her as they spun around the ballroom.

"My mother loves celebrations, and I have learned how to host one from her," Will paused to guide Emily through a turn, "you should have seen her face when I went to announce the engagement—between a grand ball and an advantageous match she likely could not be more proud."

"Was she the one in red and gold? With the dragons?" Emily asked.

Will looked down at Emily, "You have made her acquaintance?"

"No, but she is hard to miss," Emily noted. "A captivating woman," she looked back up at Will, "and this apple doesn't fall far from the tree."

Will cocked his head and went back to looking around the room as they danced, "I decided to put some effort into my appearance today. I was under the impression you might appreciate it."

Emily moved the hand that was resting on Will's shoulder and toyed with the collar of his coat, "You do clean up pretty well." She laid her hand on his chest, still looking at his face. He really was handsome. He looked so serious, but she knew he hid kindness and compassion within his hard exterior.

"Would you like to meet her?" Will went back to the original topic.

"Would Daughter of Champion like to meet her?" Emily corrected, her voice slightly disappointed.

Will bent down to whisper in her ear, "Would Emily like to meet her?"

Emily closed her eyes and took in the feeling of Will whispering her name in her ear. It sounded so nice coming from his lips, more musical than the song that continued to play around them. She came back into the moment when she almost lost her footing, "Would that be wise?"

"My mother enjoys meeting fascinating individuals," Will remarked, again giving dramatic pause as he turned Emily out, waiting to continue speaking until they were once more face to face, pulled closely together, "and you are a fascinating individual who has earned the approbation of her son. She would adore you. Though, do not expect much in the way of visible excitement—she does not easily show emotion outwardly."

"Reminds me of someone I know," Emily heard the band ending the song. She and Will bowed to each other, then bowed to those watching. Another song began and dancers filled the floor, lining up to do another dance. The couple left the ballroom and returned to the main hall. Will's eyes searched the crowd for his mother, but Emily pulled him off in Empath's direction. He was taller than most in attendance and his flaming red hair stood out among all of the colors. They found him against a wall by the front door, scanning the crowd. Emily whispered, "What did you notice when Will was giving his speech?"

"I picked up no surprise," Empath said as he continued to look past Emily and Will, "But one individual was incredibly angry when he announced the engagement. I could not distinguish the exact source. They were somewhere within the area where some vampires were congregating, but they did not read like a vampire—the emotion was more flagrant."

"And the emotion popped up specifically at the engagement piece?" Emily asked.

Empath nodded, "Almost instantaneously."

Emily looked toward where vampires were gathering. She could tell by the gray hue of most of their skin tones, as well as the fact most of them wore dark colors. "I can go see if Wit knows anything. Maybe he saw someone visibly upset." In the crowd of darkness, Emily made out two icy blue eyes staring at her—did he know she was talking about him? Her gaze fixed on him.

"Emily, should you be going over there alone?" Will asked as Emily pulled her hand away.

Emily was only just noticing that her body was moving toward Wit, pulled by some inexplicable force. With her eyes still on the vampire, she spoke over her shoulder, "I'll be fine." The air grew colder the closer she got to the group that filled the corner of the room. Mostly men, with a few female vampires scattered among them. Out of the corner of her eye, she saw a radiant light in golden fabric to her right, but she could not turn her head to look. She could only close the distance between herself and Wit's blue eyes.

Wit reached out his hand to Emily's face. He held her, with his fingers laced into her hair, and rubbed his thumb along her cheek. Emily was startled by the fact it had liquid on it, icy cold from being in contact with his skin. The fog her mind was in had cleared as Wit turned Emily's face in the direction of the light she had seen before. A blonde figure came into focus. She was wearing a flowing golden gown with lighter gold accents— all folding over itself as it cascaded toward the floor.

"It is truly you," Belle whispered as tears welled up in her eyes, "you are alright." She wrapped her arms around Emily and breathed heavily, laughing slightly as she did so.

Wit came into Emily's view as she rested her head on the woman's shoulder. He gestured his hand and nodded his head at her, indicating that she should go with it. Emily breathed, "It is. I am," and pushed the woman away.

"But you…" Belle began, then turned to look in the direction of Will, "You really chose to marry him?" She turned back to Emily and looked her in the eyes, awaiting an answer.

"We both know it is what needs to be done." Emily stated coldly.

Belle raised her chin, "Coward." The light of the candles in the chandelier bounced off her face. Quite simply, she glowed. This woman could have launched a thousand ships.

Emily was tempted to take it back, but Wit was standing behind Belle with his arms crossed and a flat expression. She hardened herself, "I am doing this for the region."

Belle took in a large breath as her eyes narrowed. Emily could see tears once again forming as Belle pressed her lips together. The woman turned to Wit, nodded, and stormed off. Not a violent storm, but a powerful, awe-inspiring storm that brought the attention of all of the vampires surrounding them.

Wit smirked at Emily and took her hand, "It had to be done." He guided her out of the crowd of onlooking guests and into a less busy area, "She planned on declaring you an imposter. She brought a liquid meant to dissolve cloaking spells to throw on you, but I convinced her not to make a scene. Besides, it would have been a complicated affair to explain the blonde hair that would have appeared and the disappearing marks on your arm.

A small amount on your face was enough to prove that this is your true visage."

"Will she be alright?" Emily asked, looking to where Belle had stormed away. There was no sign of her.

"She had given up before on her relationship with your sister," Wit said very matter-of-factly, "But was convinced she could persuade your sister if she had one more chance to talk to her—that is why she went to the palace the other night, but apparently you are not terribly convincing in your role." Wit raised a cup to his lips—Emily hadn't even seen him pick it up. He paused before he drank when he saw the concern on Emily's face, "You did not ruin your sister's relationship. Belle refuses to be a mistress and your sister is required to marry a male. Some said she could fight for marrying whomever she would like, but she already had so many opposed to her reign simply because she was human. It was not a suitable match." When Wit finally took a drink from his cup, it left a trace of red on his lips. He saw Emily watching with wide eyes. "Scared? Repulsed?"

It was Emily's turn to narrow her eyes and smirk, "Intrigued."

The next song to play from the ballroom was the minuet. Emily, recognizing the tune, turned to see a swarm making their way to the dance floor. Will appeared from the crowd and reached out for Emily's hand, "Shall we dance?"

Emily turned to Wit, who bowed politely as he said, "We will continue at a later time."

Almost every couple was on the floor. It left very little room for error, but Emily had grown so much in confidence and her practice with Empath left her well-prepared. Will's hand was comforting. He would squeeze her hand just before they would let go and smile just before they would connect again elsewhere in the line. She was so entranced she almost did not notice Empath in the mix of bodies, dancing with his partner. Daughter of Brawn looked classically stunning in black with the deep purple lace along the edges. She also looked much older and mature as she made eyes with Empath—not light, flirty eyes, but eyes that betrayed a deeper passion.

Emily realized there was something about this dance that made everyone seem this way—the going away from someone and the magnetic pull that brings you back to them. Emily saw it between Daughter of Brawn and Empath and felt it between herself and Will. She noticed it between many of the couples—not a single one could be bothered by anyone else but their dance partner, bound by some power stronger than magic.

When the song ended, all those dancing were free from their trance and began clapping for the band. Will took Emily back off to the side. She leaned against the wall, letting her bare shoulders press against the cool stone. Beads of sweat dripped from her hairline as she caught her breath and tried to steady her heartbeat.

Will pressed himself against the wall next to her and took her hand, "Am I to believe you are enjoying your first ball?" His speech was slightly labored, as if he were out of breath as well.

Emily turned toward him, keeping her left shoulder on the wall and leaning her head to rest on the stone, hoping to pull more coolness from it, "You would believe correctly. It's hard to take it all in."

Will brushed his left hand on her face. It was blissfully cool, bringing her overall temperature down almost immediately. Emily closed her eyes and rested in the moment, allowing herself to relax. She felt a slight pull from Will's hand and could feel his breath on her lips. She leaned in slightly, then heard a voice.

"Your Lordship," the voice said, "There is a matter to which you must attend."

Emily opened her eyes to see Will turned toward his footman.

"I will be there momentarily," Will said, then looked back at Emily. He gave a sad smile, but then his attention was caught by something behind her.

Emily turned to see Wit approaching. He held out his hand, "May I escort her Highness outside for some fresh air?" He asked Will.

Will looked hurt for the briefest of moments, then resigned. He said nothing, but left Emily and Wit together. Emily wanted to call out after him or to quickly run and kiss him before he got too far away, but her body would not move.

"Come, your Highness," Wit said as he gently took Emily's hand, "You would do well with some night air."

They walked outside, around to the back of the house where the carriages were parked in a line. The drivers were nowhere to be found. Wit seemed to be looking for one in particular and stopped outside a lavish black metal coach. He opened the door and helped Emily inside before going in himself.

Chapter Fourteen

"Stay," Wit said as he moved onto the bench with Emily.

"I really should be getting back," Emily felt that Will might be waiting for her in the ballroom. She reached out and rested her hand on the door handle, but she could not move beyond that.

Wit put his arm around Emily's shoulders, his gaze still focused on the front of the car. His long fingers stroked down her arm, bringing it back down to her side, "When this is all over, stay here. Stay with me."

Their legs were pressed against each other. She looked up at his face. He was so handsome with the moonlight coming through the carriage windows, bouncing off his pale skin. She was drawn to him, but resisted as best she could for fear of getting too close, "I can't. I'm a sibling. I shouldn't be here to begin with. It's her or me in this world."

Wit looked down at her and, with his free hand, stroked one finger along her jawline, bringing her chin up as he did so, "Why not you?" He brought his face close to hers, closed his eyes, and whispered, "Why save her at all? You owe her nothing."

An unknown force pulled Emily toward him. Their lips met. He put his arm around her and held her gently by the base of the neck, pulling her deeper into the kiss. His cold skin pulled the heat from hers, giving her a fluttering, tingling sensation both in her skin and her core. Never before had Emily felt such an all-encompassing passion; it was more exciting than her previous notions of love and romance. This was *it*.

She fell completely into the moment, forgetting every responsibility. There was nothing standing between her and what she wanted. She wrapped her arms around him, threading her fingers through his hair, soft and luxurious. Every point of contact between them felt like ice. The sensation, while not particularly comfortable, heightened the experience, as she could feel every inch of where their bodies were touching, only separated by cloth.

Wit pushed his body forward and Emily shifted her hips underneath him so she wouldn't hit her head on the side as she laid her body on the bench. She exhaled through her nose and made a face, laughing at the awkwardness of the movement, but when she looked back up into his eyes, she was immediately reminded of what she wanted.

They kissed passionately. Whenever Wit began to pull himself away, Emily's whole self rose up to meet him. At one point, he held his hand on her chest so she would stop. His hair was an absolute mess and the front of his cravat had been mussed. He stared down at her and whispered, "Stay."

Emily wasn't sure she wanted to answer just yet, so she pulled him back down to continue. As their lips met, Wit hunched his back so as to begin taking off his coat, undoing a series of silver buttons. As he pulled away to throw it off of his body and to remove his cravat completely, Emily got sight of a scar where his shoulder met his neck. Two punctures that had turned black with scarring and time. They were not perfectly circular, however. They tore slightly toward his chest, as though whoever had done it was not able to get a clean bite—as if Wit had attempted to escape the vampire. Wit's hand shot up to pull his shirt collar back over the scar. He paused for a moment, then completely unfastened his shirt front, removed the shirt altogether, and leaned into Emily.

The intensity of the embrace made Emily breathe heavily, catching her breath in the moments her lips were free of their icy counterparts. Her hands caressed up and down the skin of his back and shoulders. It no longer felt as if he was pulling warmth from her, but rather that she was willingly giving her heat to him. His hands reached for the front of her dress and he tore the outermost layer with only a light pull from his slender fingers. His wit was his power, but his strength was also an asset. He looked down at her once again, "I know what you want. It's me. Stay."

When Emily heard the words *It's me,* she froze. Her lips were parted and her eyes widened, staring up at Wit. The reality came flooding back. She pushed Wit away and scrambled to sit up, finally remembering to take a breath. "I—I can't," she finally managed to whisper, her wide eyes taking in the carriage around her. She was lightheaded and her mind felt foggy, but she was trying to ground herself by feeling the textures around her—the velvet of the seat, the softness of Wit's shirt still lying on the bench. She found the cool glass pane that was covered with fog from her breath and laid her hand on it.

Wit was wide-eyed and dumbfounded. He took Emily by the chin and pointed her face at himself, "Look at me." He paused, his eyes looking from one of her eyes to the other, "You deserve this. Stay with me. Be the princess you were born to be."

The proposition was tempting. Emily began to lean in to kiss Wit once again, but Daughter of Brawn's voice chimed in the back of her head, *humans are vampire playthings.* She continued to initiate the kiss, but just before her hand left the window, she tapped it lightly twice. She gave Wit one prolonged, longing kiss, then pulled away and looked downward, saying "No. I can't stay."

Wit pulled her chin up to look at him, this time more gently than the last, "You cannot stay or you will not?" His voice was seductive, luring her back in ever so slightly.

Emily looked into Wit's eyes, shocked he would not take no for an answer. Her expression hardened and she committed fully to her decision, "I will not." Her voice was firm and each word came out sharp.

Wit's expression changed to disgust as his grip on her chin tightened. With only a flick of his wrist, he threw Emily to the ground behind him.

The back of Emily's head caught the iron door handle as she fell. She blacked out for a moment, but it was one moment too long as she was awoken by the sensation of stabbing fire on the right side of her neck and a crippling cold radiating from that point. The pain was so intense that she could not even manage a scream. She willed her hands to push him away, but her fingers were too busy grasping for anything to hold on to. Her left hand found the back of her head behind her ear and her nails dug into her scalp, trying to let her feel anything but the excruciating pain she felt in that moment. Her right hand found its way to Wit's back. She weakly batted at him, but he was so much stronger. She felt her body losing energy and warmth. She sunk deeper and deeper into a sort of dream.

"Emily!" She barely heard Will's voice calling for her from somewhere outside.

She squeaked weakly, "Will!"

Wit, startled, paused in drinking the blood from her open wound. In this moment, Emily slid out from under him. He had one of her arms pinned with one hand, but once she was able to maneuver her legs free, she used her shoe heel and all of her body weight to pin to the chair the arm that was holding her. She had no idea where this energy came from. She felt stronger, sharper, and faster than she had before. In this moment of clarity, she escaped his grasp and vaulted herself over him, diving for the window portal she had created.

Wit snapped around immediately but was only able to grasp her shoe when Emily was already through the portal to her waist. She kicked her foot twice—once to shake her shoe free from Wit's grasp, and the second to shatter the window through which she had just entered.

Chapter Fifteen

Emily awoke, unaware of how long she had been unconscious. She was face down on the stone floor of her sister's room. As she tried to rise, she collapsed back to the floor. Her entire core felt frozen, so much so that the floor felt warm, even without a fire going. Her limbs were heavy and all she could do was lie where she had landed when she went through the window portal. Her left cheek was on the floor and she could see under the foot of her sister's bed. A few boxes could be seen behind the bed skirt, one ornately decorated with a mosaic of colors swirling whimsically. The longer she stared at it, the warmer it looked, as if something inside was making the colors more vibrant. They seemed to come alive and dance before her eyes as she blacked out once again.

When she awoke the second time, she was able to lift her chest off of the ground. She found a small puddle of dried blood where her head had been. She leaned onto her elbow and reached up to touch her head first, searching for the source of the blood. She felt cold, sticky wetness entangling the hair at the base of her skull behind her left ear. She brought her fingers back in front of her face and inspected it—blood. The smell made Emily's stomach turn. She shifted her balance onto her other elbow as her unbloodied right hand reached up to her shoulder—the skin around the area was clean and smooth, but the two large puncture wounds she felt had already begun to form scars. Her fingers traced a figure eight around the two marks, feeling the soft skin, gaining a sense of calm through the repetitive and predictable sensation of the self-stimulation.

Emily soon found the energy to sit up and move over to the wall for support. She dragged herself into the shards of glass that had fallen from the window when she broke it. The shards pierced her skin, though she did not bleed—*maybe there's not much blood left* she thought. The sound of glass clinking against glass and scraping against stone was near-deafening. When she finally rested against the stone wall, which felt warm to the touch, she relished the still quiet of her father's house. She tucked her thighs into her chest, laid her head on her knees, and fell asleep exhausted from that small bit of energy she had exerted.

"Emily!" Someone pounded on the door. "Emily, let me in!"

She couldn't place the voice immediately, "Who?" she managed to say. She rubbed her eyes to clear them of sleep, but her vision remained unfocused.

"Emily, it's your father. Unlock the door," the voice said. It was her dad's voice, but Emily was wary. She was weak and vulnerable right now, an easy target for anyone wanting to harm her. They knew her real name, however, so it could only be one of a handful of people.

"How do you know I'm here?" She asked, a little louder than before.

"Empath rode from the party," her dad sounded concerned, but impatient, "He felt you were in danger. He informed Will, but while they went in search of you, he could not feel you at all. He was coming to ask my assistance when he felt you in the house."

"Prove it," Emily demanded.

From the other side of the door Empath's voice piped up, "You were," he paused a moment, "enamored," he paused again to clear his throat, "then defiant, scared, terrified, empowered momentarily, then gone completely. I thought you had been killed. Now I feel you once again and you are confused and scared. Cold, as well. Very cold. I'll fetch fire."

Emily lifted her head and stared at the door, concentrating. She flicked her finger up, bringing the metal bar out of its latch. The door immediately swung open, revealing the large figure of her father taking up the entire doorway. She saw his eyes go from the floor in front of him to the puddle of blood to the shattered glass to Emily herself, pausing on each one to take in the situation. By the time he had seen the torn-apart dress and the marks on her shoulder, the look on his face was that of absolute horror.

Emily took a shuddering breath and whispered, "Dad." She burst into tears. The wind whipped through the open window, throwing tapestries off of the walls and slamming the door wide open. Champion pushed through the onslaught of wind and made his way over to her, wrapping his arms around her. She instantly felt the warmth of his body that she could never feel before. This warmth was not comforting, though. The ice in her veins was still painfully cold. Thunder roared outside. He picked her up in his huge arms and put her down by the fireplace. He stroked the dark hair on her head comfortingly.

Empath entered carrying Daughter of Brawn's fire bag. He held the bottom and tilted the top toward the fireplace, letting three fireballs topple out. The fireplace was sent into a frenzy of flames and sparks. He jumped back to avoid the fire's spit and turned toward Emily with his fair face reflecting the red flames, expressionless, "It was Wit, wasn't it?"

Emily could only nod, still an absolute mess of tears with gasping breaths in between. The tears that fell down her cheeks were just as cold as she was. She was getting her energy back, but it was all going toward this emotional release.

Empath's eyes were wide and concerned, "Will is still there looking for you. He will tear himself apart if he thinks anything has happened to you."

Through stuttered, sobbing breaths, Emily was able to let out, "You give him—too much—credit. He—will only care—that his plan—failed." She paused to take a deeper breath and planted her head into her father's chest, "That I failed."

Empath's eyes fell to the floor, "It is you who gives him too little credit, Highness." Champion shot Empath a stern, fatherly glare, but Empath continued, "I apologize, Your Majesty, but he cares for Emily—in a different way than he cares for your other daughter, but just as strong. He needs to know she is safe."

Emily felt lighter with that revelation, but it was immediately replaced by dread, "What if Wit already found him? What if he follows him here?" She was no longer sobbing, she was focused, "I need to go find him." She tried to get up, pushing herself out of her father's arms, but collapsed back onto the floor in front of the fire.

Champion wrapped his arms around his daughter and pulled her into his chest once again, "You need to rest."

The painful chill was still stabbing into her core and neither the fire nor her father's warmth did anything to help. She wished her hands had gone numb, but instead her skin felt like needles were digging into every inch. Her eyelids were weighted, her neck weak. *Is this what hypothermia feels like?* She gave in and let her eyes close. Before she drifted off to sleep once again, she heard Daughter of Brawn's voice talking to Empath. She wanted to acknowledge her friend but could not bring her body to use her voice or lift her head.

The next time period was a blur of sounds and feelings Emily was vaguely aware of conversations, being moved to a bed, the windows closing, water pouring, but the whole time never being alone as she felt warmth from hands that held her own, squeezed her shoulder, and stroked her hair. She wanted to engage, but everything was happening so quickly, each event had ended by the time she could make sense of it. The sound of the shutters opening again was the moment Emily's mind was finally able to keep up. Her senses keyed into the specifics going on around her. She was lying on a bed, her head sunken into soft pillows. It was night—the cool air rushed in the windows and cut through the staleness caused by a group of people being shut into a room for an entire day. Emily heard three steps and felt a hand once more on hers. It was warm. The warmth itself brought no comfort, however, the fact that the hand was there did.

She could hear Empath whisper in the corner, "She's awake." Two metal chairs scraped on the stone floor and two sets of feet started toward her—one in long strides and the other in short, hurried steps. A third chair in the other far corner groaned as its heavy occupant rose. This last sound brought Emily pause. She thought her father was the one holding her hand, but who else would be large enough to cause that much strain on a cast iron chair?

She opened her eyes to see Empath and Daughter of Brawn smiling at the foot of the bed, her father standing in the far corner looking on anxiously, and Will holding onto Emily's hand and giving a full-bodied sigh of relief.

He leaned in and kissed her cheek. "It's me," he whispered, then added as he pulled away to sit back down, "How do you feel?"

Emily checked in with herself. The cold pain had subsided and was now just incredibly uncomfortable. Her head was clear. Her energy had returned almost fully. She reached up and felt the crusted blood in her hair, but there was no pain from the wound that produced it or from where she had been bitten. "I feel," her face contorted, "fine."

The whole room let out a sigh of both relief and concern. Will and Champion locked eyes while Daughter of Brawn and Empath looked back and forth between the two.

As Emily was growing uncomfortable in the silence, Daughter of Brawn finally piped in, "We drew a bath for you in the next room and have been keeping it warm. Perhaps we will all feel better after some freshening up." She came to Emily's side and helped her out of the bed. After throwing a cloak over Emily's shoulders and tying it in the front to cover her torn and bloodied dress, Daughter of Brawn snuck Emily into the bathroom the next door over. Emily saw steam rising from the tub that was located in the middle of the room. She hoped it would do something to warm her, but had the sinking feeling it would do nothing.

Daughter of Brawn helped untie the cloak and asked, "Would you like me to stay or go?"

"I'd like you to stay, since I feel like I missed something," Emily saw the screen in the corner and gestured to it, "but I'd also like a bit of privacy."

Daughter of Brawn nodded, helped unbutton the back of Emily's destroyed dress, and made her way behind the curtain. When she was situated, she asked hesitantly, "What exactly do you want to know?"

Emily dipped her toes into the just-below-boiling water. She felt it scald her skin, but the warmth did not stay once she took her foot back out. She got into the tub completely and could feel a slight warmth travel through her muscles and into her core, but it disappeared when it hit the icy rock in the center. Emily turned her attention back to Daughter of Brawn's question, "Can you just state the obvious first? I think I can put two and two together, but I need someone else to say it."

There was a silence from behind the screen, followed by a short sniffle before Daughter of Brawn said, "It has been over one hundred years since anyone with human blood has been bitten. We can't be sure…" Her voice trailed off.

Emily's bath water had cooled considerably in the mere moments she had been in it. It was still warm, but nowhere near where it was when she had gotten in. She rubbed her bite wound, removing the bit of crusted blood that covered each puncture. She was becoming frustrated with her companion, "Can't be sure of *what*? Please just say it."

Daughter of Brawn sobbed from the other side of the screen, "Why would you ask him to do this, Emily?"

Emily turned to face the screen so quickly that a wave of water cascaded out of the side of the tub, "Ask him?" She yelled. Her voice echoed in every corner of the room. She paused as the echo subsided and she gathered her temper, "I didn't ask him to bite me. He attacked me."

There was another pause from behind the screen. While Daughter of Brawn said nothing, Emily could sense an *'I told you so'* that wanted to be said. Instead, Daughter of Brawn began speaking at an uncharacteristically slow pace, "Will thought as much. Wit told him that you had asked to be changed so you would have to stay here, but then you got scared part way through and ran. They went looking for you together."

Emily, who had been rubbing water into her hair to clean out the dried blood, paused, "Wit is here?" As she asked, she noticed that her hair was once again its normal blonde color. She smiled, realizing that someone had changed it back while she was sleeping.

"No. Your father would not let him in; he was furious. Wit left as the sun rose."

"But he knows I'm here?" The water Emily was bathing in had become cold. She didn't mind it, but would have preferred to have continued sitting in warm water.

"He does, Highness," Daughter of Brawn paused, "I should tell Will this information in case Wit returns—make sure no one allows him inside the palace." Emily heard her footsteps on the stone floor as she went to leave the room.

Emily did not protest, but instead dunked her head under the water. She stayed under the water, enjoying the quiet, but had no urge to surface. She remained submerged for a minute, two minutes before she stopped counting. There was no panic, no innate need to breathe. She waited for the moment her lungs would start to ache, but she realized that moment was not going to come. She surfaced and filled her lungs, not out of necessity, but out of habit.

Emily pushed her soaked hair from her forehead and brought her arms out in front of her. They no longer showed her sister's markings. She looked at her skin in the lamplight. There was no pink or peach left in its hue. Her skin had greyed like Wit's. All life had left her coloring. Daughter of Brawn would not admit it, but it appeared to Emily as if she was no longer human. She had been bitten by a vampire and now must be one herself—there was no other explanation. Voices were in the next room, separated from Emily by a stone wall, but when she focused on the words, Emily could hear the conversation as if they were right next to her.

"We need to keep him off her track until we can figure out what we are going to do," Will's voice paused, "This is my fault. I let them go off together."

Empath's voice came next, "You could not have known this would happen."

"I all but told her to go with him," Will said, a little more unsteadily, "I needed to prove something to myself."

"That you could let her go?" Empath asked.

"She was never mine to begin with," Will stumbled on his words, "but now she cannot go. I told her she would get to go home."

"You do not want her to go," Empath stated in the blank tone he used when he was reading someone.

"No, but now she has no choice," Will said angrily just before a door slammed and footsteps made their way down the hallway.

Emily was sitting in icy cold water. She dried off and found some clothes folded on a chair—one of the high-waisted gowns that was easy to move in. She tried to dry her hair by generating warmth in her hands, but something was stopping her powers from working. She laid her wet hair down the right side of her neck to cover the scar. *If* she had truly become a vampire, that would be a long-term problem that would have to wait. There were more immediate concerns.

She entered her sister's room once more. It was evident she had interrupted whisperings between Empath and her father, "Don't stop on my account," she said as she closed the door, "But when you have a minute I'd like to discuss elves."

The two stared at her for a few moments before Daughter of Brawn nudged Empath, who straightened, "What exactly would you care to know, your Highness?"

Emily looked at him. He seemed so out of place here with his radiant skin and red hair, but he was exactly who she needed right now, "I need you to map out the location of every elven clan you know of."

Chapter Sixteen

By the time Will arrived back at the palace, the dining room table was cluttered with maps and books. Emily had quickly become proficient in quill use as she marked suspected locations and notations on the largest map. Empath could not give many specifics, but could give approximations and details from stories he was told as a child and Emily jotted them down as quickly as he could remember them.

The only location he could give with moderate certainty, however, was that of his own clan. Since it was so close to the Dark Region, Emily knew it was where she would go first. Empath warned, "You will not be able to see the entrance to the caverns unless they allow you to. They will know you are there long before you realize you are in the correct location. You can tell them I sent you and they may be more apt to open the doors, but I cannot guarantee they will give you an audience."

"I need to try. I really have no other choice," Emily admitted. Champion and Daughter of Brawn were pulling books in from the library—anything they had on elves, the Mountains, and potions. Emily only noticed Will had entered when the door shut behind him. She walked over to him and gestured toward the table, "We don't have a lot of time left. We obviously found

170

out nothing at the party, so we have to start with plan B. Someone had to make the potion; we just have to find out who so we can ask for an antidote."

"You should be resting," Will furrowed his brow and ran his hand down Emily's arm, holding her hand as he came to it, "Are you well enough to be walking around?"

"I am great, actually," Emily said excitedly, "Besides this lingering, all-encompassing cold, I feel amazing. I could take on the world if I needed to."

"Good, I suppose," Will spoke hesitantly, as if he did not quite believe that Emily could have recovered so quickly. He changed the topic, "I told Wit that you were still asleep. He said that when he had converted humans before it could take an entire week before they awoke. I told him that I would notify him immediately of any changes. He seemed to believe me."

Emily nodded—Wit was not her concern at the moment, but in the back of her mind she did feel the need to know why he had done this. She would confront him if there was the opportunity, but her mission was to save her sister and time was running out.

Over the course of the night, plans were finalized—Emily and Will would travel into the Mountains together via a portal, but the elves would not be receptive to more than one stranger entering their area, so Emily would have to travel the last portion of the journey alone. Empath would not be able to accompany her, either, as he was not allowed to return to his clan for twenty years. If he tried, they might cast him out for twenty years more, or possibly never allow him to return at all.

Daughter of Brawn modified some clothes to be more suitable for hiking up mountains—making a skirt into pantaloons that would be worn with boots so as to completely cover her legs as she trekked through vegetation. She found and modified a sleek leather coat to protect Emily's arms while still allowing for mobility. She would also wear a cloak to protect her head and neck from any sunlight.

She would start with Empath's clan, then inquire about the three other clans for which they pieced together the general location. The hope was that each clan would have information about the others that they would be willing to disclose should they believe Emily's story. She would have to be honest with the elves, as they had ways of discovering the truth.

They planned to begin their journey after the Dark region's sunset when the sun would be low in the Mountain sky. Will would stay over in one of the guest rooms so he would not have a chance meeting with Wit in the meantime. Emily went to her sister's room and laid on the bed. She was not tired—she was not sure if she even needed sleep anymore.

Visions of vampire media snapped into her head. Old Dracula film reels and contemporary vampire slayer scenes of a damsel in distress with a handsome, pale man slowly creeping in to bite her neck. Why had she blocked these from her mind? They could have served as cautionary tales. She would be stuck here, unable to hide vampire qualities and impulses in the human world; a creature of seduction and death.

After a long day of half-sleep and a combination of daydreams and nightmares, there was a knock on the door.

Her father entered and immediately wrapped his arms around her, "I am sorry we let this happen to you. You are welcome to stay after all of this is over—whether or not you manage to save your sister." He grabbed her by the shoulders and held her away so he could look in her eyes, "I will fight to let you stay. I should have fought harder before, and I have regretted it every day since."

"They would have killed me," Emily reminded him, "You saved me and mom. We had a good life and she knew you loved us." She put her hand on his arms that were bridged between them. She could feel his warmth through his shirt.

Champion continued to look at Emily a while before he coughed, obviously holding back some emotions. He blinked quickly, remembering something, "Just a moment." He fell to the floor and tried to wriggle under the bed. He was so large he could not slide under, so he lifted the entire metal frame with one hand and squeezed his other hand far enough to grab something. He pulled out the ornate box that Emily had seen the night before. He blew off the dust that had collected since it was last opened, "I had this made for your mother to keep with her and gave it to your sister when she was old enough. It can protect you from vampires. Your sister never carried it, so I did not believe you would need it. I wish I would have given it to you yesterday, but now you can protect yourself in case he comes back. I do not trust him."

"Neither do I," Emily half-chuckled. She was surprised how little she felt toward him now. She should have been devastated, heartbroken over being betrayed by someone she felt so strongly toward, but now she simply did not care. It was as if it was a stranger who had attacked her and the only emotion she had toward him was resentment.

She opened the box to find a beautiful dagger with a silver hilt encrusted with red gems. It rested in a dark leather scabbard. She pulled the blade out—it appeared to be a normal weapon. Perhaps it was enchanted? She admired it from a few different angles. When she looked directly down the point, she noticed the middle of the blade was much thicker than the edges.

"The first stab can only injure," Champion said as he took the weapon and slid the blade back into its scabbard, "But the second will kill." He used both hands to present the dagger to Emily, who placed it in the bag that was with her traveling clothes.

Emily didn't know what she would encounter out there. She was not sure the elves would be receptive—or if they would even allow a vampire to exist anywhere near their home. Empath told her how much his own clan distrusted the vampires, and they had what was considered one of the better relationships. She told the truth when she said she could take on the world—she could take on *her* world, but *this* world held dangers she didn't even know about yet, especially now that she was venturing out of the relative security of this region.

"I wish you didn't have to go alone."

Emily fiddled with her clothes for the next day, facing away so her father wouldn't see her reservations so plain on her face, "You all have to stay to keep Wit off our trail."

Champion did not respond. His silence was almost deafening until there was a knock on the door—Will was ready to go. Champion finally grumbled, "I will see you when you get back."

On her way to the door, Emily hugged her father one last time. She couldn't say a word, too afraid of breaking down. She would have to be strong right now. She would have to be strong until she brought her sister back. She could fall apart when this was all over.

Will was dressed in just a shirt and vest with some well-worn breeches. It was the most dressed-down Emily had ever seen him. He seemed more relaxed in those clothes, but his face was stern. Something was bothering him and he couldn't get past it. He took Emily to an empty room and shut the door behind him, "Bringing two people is going to take a great deal of energy. I can take you to the Mountains, but I will not be able to travel much further without resting. You will be doing most of this alone."

With a nod, Emily readjusted the satchel that carried the dagger. "I'm ready. Let's do this."

After an incantation, a dark circle opened in the air before them. The color was darker than darkness itself—as if all light had ceased to exist in that space. Will gestured toward it, "Ladies first."

Emily lifted a booted foot into the bottom edge of the circle. As she moved forward, her toe disappeared into a plane of black, then her foot, then her entire leg. She threw the second half of her body through, feeling a rush of emptiness as her head went through the void. She fell to her knees, sharp rocks from a gravel road pressing into her flesh. The setting sun scalded her forehead in the moment before she raised the hood of her cloak to block it. As she rose from the ground, she brushed off her pants and looked at the landscape off to her left.

Will fell to the ground next to her just as the dark circle snapped shut behind them. He was not as quick to get up. He lay on his side taking heaving breaths. If she had not been looking at him, she might not have even noticed he was there—he suffered in silence.

Emily rubbed his back, "Hey, are you going to be ok?"

Will looked up at Emily, confused, "Did it not try to stop you?" His whispered words took focused effort.

The backrub paused, "No," Emily matched his confusion, "What would have tried to stop me?"

"I do not know," Will tried to sit up, but almost immediately reconsidered and laid his head back on the road, "Something pushed me back. I had to reopen the portal and force my way through." He laid looking up at the sky, "Something does not want me here."

"Well, I want you here," the words felt strange as she said them, "I'm not doing all of this alone." She had done so much on her own in the past few years she couldn't have imagined needing a team this badly.

The mountains stood before her—sharp, glacial peaks in the distance and tall, intimidating foothills immediately before her. There were well-defined layers in the vegetation—grasses at the bottom led to bright green shrubs that clung to the rock like moss. Another few hundred feet and the vegetation no longer grew, but harsh, black rock took its place. Atop those rocks was a light dusting of snow. She could barely make out a stretch of fog on the horizon, far to her left.

The scenery was so distracting, Emily did not notice Will getting to his feet behind her. She only realized he was there when his arms reached around her shoulders and he kissed her on the cheek, "It's me."

They stood there a moment, Emily supporting Will as he half-rested on her. She could feel him catching his breath. When she felt he had mostly recovered, she turned to face him.

Will looked into Emily's eyes, "I am afraid I do not have the energy to go any further."

"This is really where you're leaving me? You can't even go with me into the foothills?" Emily looked back pleadingly.

"I cannot," he whispered, "this you must do alone." He grabbed both her hands and looked as if he was about to say something, but then broke eye contact and looked at the hills behind her, "Find the river and follow it toward the source. Where three rivers converge is where they're said to live. Look for the signs Empath told you about. I will be here when you get back." He squeezed her hands and let go, stepping back as if to walk away.

She looked up at the tall, cold mountain looming in the distance. Her gaze drifted to the gentle green grasses that filled the ground in front of her. She could see the dew on each blade. She heard the trickle of the stream cutting through the rocky ground. The crispness called to her. The air was moist, but light. The color green was overwhelming after being without it for so long and Emily was drawn to it. She walked off the road and went to lay down in the grass. The clean, sharp smell surrounded her. She turned her face and felt the dew on her cheek. She felt at home for a moment, like she was lying in the park just after sunset, until she felt pain. Each blade of grass that touched her skin felt like a hot knife stabbing into her flesh. She screamed a horrible shriek. She could hear a hiss as the moisture boiled out of her skin, letting off steam.

Will had obviously not gone far, as he was there almost immediately to help lift her up. She was paralyzed with pain. "You fool," He embraced her tightly. Everywhere he touched was cooled immediately. She barely noticed the relief under the excruciating pain. She buried her face in his shoulder and screamed. There was nothing else she could do.

When she was able to compose herself, she pushed away and looked up into Will's face. His black eyes were glistening. He reached for her cheek and caressed it. The pain left, but the sensation she felt wasn't skin on skin. She reached her fingers up to feel for herself. Part of her cheek was crusted with a hard, rough layer. Will put his hand over hers, "Please be careful. Stay out of the sun and away from plants. You are stronger now, but also vulnerable in new and different ways." He reached around her head to undo her hair so it fell over her shoulders, a blonde cascade covering the skin on her neck. He reached for her hair again, but this time he held his hand back there to pull Emily in to kiss her on the lips. It felt every bit as exciting and passionate as the kiss with Wit, but also felt tender and safe. She sunk into his lips completely.

He pulled away his lips, but rested his forehead on hers, "I need you to stay safe." He whispered.

Emily pulled slightly away, realizing the weight of what just happened, "For my sister."

Will pulled her back toward him, lightly enough that she could pull away if she wanted to, but she allowed herself to rest against him again as he responded, "For me."

Emily was breathless. Nobody had cared for her in so long, but the whole purpose of this adventure was to save the person to whom he was promised. For now, she was off on her own in the wilderness and someone wanted her to come back. She lifted her face to kiss him again and walked away without speaking, avoiding the grass and still tasting his lips on hers.

Chapter Seventeen

Emily followed the river into the mountains as darkness fell. It was wide and slow where she joined the water, but the higher she walked the faster the current ran. It led her into a narrow gorge in the foothills. The steep sides were covered with grasses and shrubs with collections of rocks scattered throughout—some looked like they could fall on her at any moment. The land looked new—volcanic with young growth. She did not know if she could make it to her destination before sunrise, but the mountains would give her protection from the sun's direct rays for a long while. She would only have to worry around midday when the sun would come over the peaks. For now, a comforting darkness engulfed the valley. With no lights or fire to guide her, Emily began to worry about the impending gloom, but as light departed, she realized she was still able to see incredibly well. Colors were still vibrant; details were still crisp. Daylight no longer served a purpose when warmth and light were meaningless.

When the flora met the river, Emily was forced to wade into the water to avoid touching vegetation as she clambered up the hillside. The water rushed into her boots instantly. It was glacial—Emily had foolishly swum in freshly melted glacial water before and remembered the icy bite. This chill did not hurt, though. It did not produce the stabbing feeling that near-freezing cold had before. There was no "getting used to" the water temperature. It was simply cold.

As she gained in elevation, Emily attempted to use her powers. She stopped a few times to help her focus. The earth did not move for her. Fire was no longer conjurable. Was this because she was no longer in the Dark region? Was there a sort of limit on her power around elven lands? Was her body still recovering from the bite? Or did her power simply no longer exist? Emily considered all of the possibilities, but could not mourn her lack of powers. She could only mentally prepare for entering a magical clan's lair without any means of defense.

Emily eventually came to the top of her first foothill—a viewpoint from which she could see the river's entire course from the larger mountain on the other side of a dale. She would have to venture down then up again, about to her current elevation. It was there she would find the meeting of three rivers. She wished she could just walk across the air or jump the thousands of feet to her destination.

Feeling a rush of adrenaline, Emily set her feet and focused her eyes on her destination. She took off running down the hill with a speed she had never reached before. Shrubs tore at her pantaloons, threatening to burn her skin, but she was too fast to let the vegetation sit on her flesh long enough to cause damage. When she got to the grassy layer, she felt as if she would slow down due to the shallower slope of the ground, but instead she picked up speed, feeling a surge of momentum. Air pressed hard against her face and body, whipping her cloak behind her like a flag in a storm. She kept up her sprint even as she began to scale the steep grade. Instead of fumbling over the various rocks and crevasses, Emily soared over them in long bounds, leaping effortlessly from foothold to foothold.

It took her only a quarter of the time to climb the second mountain as it had the first and she needed no time to catch her breath. She had reached the meeting of the three rivers. The rightmost river rushed quickly and violently, churning white, foamy crests. The middle river carried minerals from the top of the mountain; dark reds and browns swirled through its current. The river on the left was so clear she could see each rock at the bottom. The point where they merged was a work of art. The clear and brown rivers pressed together in sharp contrast while the rough river pushed them into swirling eddies. Emily was in awe of its beauty as a piece of art, created by some magical being. Perhaps they were inspired by true nature, by whatever forces had created her world, but this was intentionally set in place.

Emily knew she would not need to follow the clear river—it held no secrets. The mineral river could have promise, leading to a place that was rich in life-bringing elements, but was that what she was looking for? The violent river crashed, throwing itself against the banks. The sound held Emily's attention. It held great power, caused great change, and could execute great destruction. She veered right, keeping her eyes down to look for some of the signs that Empath told her would indicate that she was getting close. Out of the corner of her eye, she spotted one—tiny white flowers, trailing in a line. The hillside had been covered with these flowers, but only in concentrated spots or random groups. Here, it appeared they had been painted in swirls and streaks. Emily searched for some sort of opening. She found nothing but more hillside, despite her certainty that she was in the right place.

"Hello?" She called out to the emptiness, "I need your help."

Her call echoed off the mountains, sending her voice back to her in staggered pleas.

"I was sent by Empath…" Emily paused, trying to remember how to pronounce the name he had told her before she left, "…by Lathron." The Mountains did not adhere to the same naming conventions as the Dark region. Empath had been given a name by his own kind, but was forced to abandon it when he left his home.

Emily waited in the dark. The river behind her raged, masking all other sounds. A moon rose above the hills, shining a silvery glow on the surface of each leaf and each blade of grass before her. This moon was familiar—it looked almost identical to the Earth's moon. She could see the man in the moon. She could make out the rabbit from the storybook her mom used to read to her. Emily laid down her cloak and sat on it, admiring the beauty of the night. There was nothing to do now but wait to see if she would be allowed to meet with the elves.

A deep voice cut through the ambient noise, "Why should we help a vampire?"

Emily turned quickly to see a tall, lean figure standing right behind her. As she rose, she could see he had a stern expression, laced with impatience. His long white hair blew gently and his pale skin seemed to glow. Emily shielded her eyes from the brightness, "Because I was human only a few nights ago. Because I need to help my sister. Because the stability of the Dark region depends on there being an heir."

The elf closed his eyes for a few moments, as if listening carefully for something. Emily heard nothing, but when the elf opened his eyes he nodded. Without a word, he turned and began walking up alongside the river, toward a waterfall that had not been there when Emily last looked. Emily scrambled to pick up her cloak and secure it once more around her neck as she trailed behind the graceful figure. He waded into the river and stepped through the waterfall, disappearing from view. Emily stepped into the water, the current attempting to pull her legs out from under her. She took slow, steady steps. She passed under the wall of water, only to find a stone wall behind it. She reached out to touch it, but found her hand moving through it instead. She stepped through, feeling a rush of warmth as she entered into the hidden space.

The room was filled with elves—at least five pointing staffs at her, others taking her belongings. The staffs were wooden with a point at the end. They were all pointed directly at her chest. *A wooden stake to the heart.* Though they did not touch her, she could feel their piercing heat just by looking at them. The glowing elf was speaking to another being with red hair that was reminiscent of her friend's. She knew she was in the right place.

The elf who had taken her bag presented Emily's dagger to the redhead. He inclined his head, holding the dagger up to the light. The rubies took in the torchlight that lit the room and cast out red reflections onto the elf's face. His face was unamused as he cast his gaze on Emily, "Curious you should carry the means of your own demise." He tossed the dagger back to the elf with the bag, "Leave her belongings here. She means us no harm. Take her to my chambers."

A set of hands grabbed each of Emily's arms, pushing her down a long cavern. She initially tried to resist but realized this was exactly what she wanted—to meet with them in private.

The tunnel sloped down, further into the depths of the mountain. Through doorways Emily saw large, empty rooms and halls, somehow lit by the same silvery light that was given off by the outside moon. It was eerily quiet, save the drips of water leaking from the stones above her and the footsteps of her and her guards.

They continued through a large room with huge windows. The night sky could be seen outside, yet there was no evidence of this large palace from above ground. The moonlight illuminated stone walls upon which ivy grew. There were water features in each corner—waterfalls gushing huge amounts of water that became mist as it fell, disappearing before hitting the dry floor. The guards pulled Emily into a small room off of the main hall.

The red-haired elf was already sitting at a wooden table. The room was filled with wooden furniture. The shelves that covered the walls were filled with scrolls wrapped around shining golden and silver rollers. The elf gestured to the wooden seat opposite him, but Emily shook her head, "I believe I would be more comfortable standing."

"Have you brought word of my son?" The elf asked once the guards left the room, leaning forward in his chair, "How does he fare?"

"Em—Lathron?" Emily quickly corrected herself.

"You say he sent you," Empath's father stood, "You must have word of his well-being."

"Of course," Emily fumbled into the pockets and pulled out a small, steel ring, "He told me to give this to you and it would explain everything." She held it out to him in the palm of her hand.

He took the ring and studied it. He read the engraving on the inside, turning it as he went. He continued to rotate it well past the point he should have run out of words, but his expression showed he was still taking in new information. After a few minutes, he smiled at Emily, "Fascinating. I ask that you call me Carandol." He placed the ring on his desk and moved closer to Emily, circling her like a hawk. He eyed her up and down, "How long ago were you bitten?"

Emily wasn't sure if she should follow him with her eyes or stare straight ahead, so she compromised by eyeing him only when he was in front of her, "Two nights past."

"We can reverse this," he stopped directly in front of Emily, "If you would like your humanity restored."

Emily faltered, "No, that's...that's not what I'm here for," she paused, realizing the full gravity of what he had said, "You can?"

"We have a way to restore your humanity, yes," Carandol turned away from Emily, searching for a scroll on a shelf nearby,

"It is not without risk, however, and you will become completely human—no longer part demon or vampire."

"So I would have to go home?" Emily asked with a hint of disappointment, realizing that *home* was not a good word for it anymore, "Back to the human world?"

"Yes," he said dismissing her reservations, focused on his hunt, "The scroll is here somewhere. We have not had use for it in ages, but it can be located."

Emily remembered her primary objective, "I need to know if you have created a Vengeful Sleep potion recently."

Carandol stormed to the door, "Guards!" Two elves appeared; they had been waiting on each side of the door. He whispered some words in an unfamiliar language and the blond guard rushed off. Carandol began to speak to the second, a bulkier elf with brown hair, but paused to go back to his table and write down long, slender letters on some parchment. He returned to the guard and handed it to him. The second guard nodded and hurried away. Carandol turned back to Emily, "That question is best left for our potion master. He will be here shortly." He sat back down at his desk and leaned forward with interest, "Until then, tell me about what led you to this moment."

Emily gave a brief version of her story, emphasizing the role Empath played so as to keep his father's interest. The elf seemed to have not heard from his son in a long while. He asked clarifying questions to confirm that he had, indeed, been named and that his powers were developing. Before Emily could mention her excitement about the nature of Empath and Daughter of Brawn's relationship, another elf came in the room. The elves all looked so similar. The shape of their faces, the angle of their eyes—there was hardly any variation in their appearance besides hair color, eye color, and overall build, like they had all been built using the same template. It seemed as if there was little genetic diversity in this clan. Perhaps it would be wise to not mention his son's affection for someone so unlike his own kind.

The new elf wore flowing robes and walked with a staff. He seemed older than Carandol, but Emily could only see this through the slight wrinkles around his eyes and the limp with which he walked. His hair was grey with silver running through it. He was clearly upset, "Carandol, you wake me in the middle of the night," he growled with a raspy voice, "You must have good reason."

Carandol bowed to his elder, "Master, we have a guest who is only available during the night, otherwise she would have been made to wait."

The old elf glared at Emily, "A vampire," he scoffed, "I am done with vampires."

"You may wish to reconsider," Carandol walked over to him and said something in the unknown language. The older elf's eyes widened as he looked Emily over. When Carandol stepped back away, he gestured to Emily, "Daughter of Champion, I present our master of potions, Daeron."

Emily curtsied, unsure of what to do with her hands as she had no skirt to lift out of the way, "I do not mean to be rude, but time is not on my side. I need to know if you've brewed a Vengeful Sleep potion recently."

Daeron rested his weight on his staff, holding it in both hands, "Yes, and I was under the assumption you were the victim, being the only known part-human in the realm. However, the hair used was brown, not yellow as yours is." His glassy eyes were fixed on Emily.

Excitement bubbled up inside her as she realized it was a good sign for her sister's prognosis, "Is there an antidote?"

"No," the potion master said as his voice hushed, "There is only one way to reverse the potion—to kill the one whose blood sought vengeance before the fifteenth morning."

Emily stepped forward. She only needed one more piece of information, "Who did you brew the potion for?"

"Are you certain that this is the question you wish to ask?" Daeron turned and gave Emily a sidelong glance.

She reconsidered only for a moment—she needed this information, no matter who it ended up being, "Yes. Who did you brew the potion for?" she repeated.

"A vampire. I did not get his name. Light hair, tall. Arrogant."

Emily felt a kick in the gut as she realized she knew exactly who it was. The feeling intensified when she realized that Wit had all but told her he hated her sister, hated humans. He wanted her to stay and had made her into a vampire to ensure that no human was on the throne. Her head began to spin as she reached out her hand for something to support her. She stumbled against the wooden shelf and recoiled immediately as she felt a searing pain on her hand.

As Carandol helped Emily to her feet, the second guard returned with a scroll on stone rollers. He made sure Emily could stand on her own before taking the scroll and opening it on his desk, "Master Daeron, how long would it take for you to make this potion?"

Daeron limped over to the scroll, looked up at Emily, then back down at the text, "No need. I still have a vial from the last time we created it."

"Do you think she is strong enough?" Carandol asked, concerned.

"She is young," the old elf noted, looking over Emily once again, "Strong, as well. So long as she has not bitten anyone, the vampire blood should be easy enough to convert. Once she drinks the blood of another, I am afraid it will be too dangerous. Since she was originally only half-demon, that should also be a simple conversion. She will likely survive," he looked back to Carandol, "but I can never make a guarantee."

"I haven't," Emily piped up, startling the two elves who seemed to have forgotten the subject of their conversation was sentient, "Bitten anyone, that is."

From his long robes, Daeron pulled a small, round-bottomed flask containing a pink liquid. He held it out to Emily with pale, knobby fingers, "Drink this if you wish to become completely human." Without another word, he hobbled out of the room and the door shut behind him.

"If you save your sister, it must be done," Carandol said after he confirmed they were alone once again. "There can only be one of you here, and this will ensure there is no magical blood in the human world."

"My father said I could stay," Emily explained. "He would fight for me to stay."

"We both know it is a fight that will only lead to chaos," Carandol came closer so they could speak in more hushed tones, "There is a reason beings of that region have but one child, especially in nobility and royalty. They will hunt down the sister they believe to be the worse choice for the realm."

"Who will?" Emily whispered, realizing that this was a conversation for just the two of them.

"Anyone with anything to gain from one of you being in power over the other."

"But he said he would fight for me," Emily insisted stubbornly.

"Is that a fight you want to put your father through? Keeping your mother safe almost killed him the first time, now he would have to protect both you and your sister." His voice became quieter, pleading, "My son is in that house, sworn to your family. You risk his life, too. You risk the life of every being in that palace. In exchange for all I have done for you tonight, do the right thing and protect your region."

Emily thought of Empath. She thought of Daughter of Brawn. She thought of every other member of the house staff.

She thought of her sister who she just wanted to keep from dying; would it all be worth it if she might put her right back in harms' way? She nodded, resolute. "There can only be one." She looked down at the vial in her hand. The glass was still warm, "But I can't do it now. I have to kill the vampire who did this to my sister first, and I can't do that as a human."

Carandol held Emily firmly by the arms, just above her elbows, and looked into her eyes. She could tell he was not adept at showing outward emotion, but was making an effort. "Thank you." His relief was palpable in his voice alone, but the shine of tears welling in his eyes nearly broke what was left of Emily's heart. How unfair it was that he would have to be separated from his son for so long, to worry for twenty years before he would even see him again. She gave him a few more awkward smiles and nods before he finally released her, walked her back down the hall, gave her her things, and sent her on her way back through the foothills.

Chapter Eighteen

Even though she ran the entire way back to Will's location, it was still almost daybreak in the Mountains before she reached him. She found him sitting with a book, almost exactly where she had left him. He rose to his feet when he saw her and she could see his smile from the mountainside. Her momentum when she reached him nearly knocked him over as she immediately kissed him. He stood strong, planting one foot behind him, and returned the affection.

When Emily got over the initial shock of her own behavior, she hesitated momentarily before revealing, "We have to kill Wit. He was the one who ordered the potion for my sister and the only antidote is to kill the one whose blood sought vengeance."

It was Will's turn to be shocked. After reflecting on this information for a minute, he collapsed onto the ground, his legs too tired to hold him. Emily sat with him and told him everything that had happened. Afterwards, they sat in silence for a long while. As the sun rose, Emily turned her back to it and raised the hood of her cloak to protect herself. Will looked off into the Mountains, too shocked to say anything. He finally whispered, "We have to kill Wit." His face was stoic, but Emily knew he must have been in turmoil finding out his friend had not only bitten Emily, but was also the one who tried to kill his fiancée.

"I can do it," Emily put her hand on Will's knee, "so you don't have to. I have a plan and the motivation right now, but it has to be done as soon as possible."

Will's dazed eyes finally found Emily's face, "You can do it."

Emily wasn't sure if he really believed that, or if he was simply repeating what she had said. She looked into his face, trying to be considerate of how he was feeling, but also trying to invoke a sense of urgency, "I need you to take me to his place right now."

"You will not be able to stay," The tone of his voice was more than just sad—he was genuinely disappointed and unable to conceal it.

Emily scrunched up her face, fighting back tears, "No, I won't," she managed to squeak out while her voice broke.

He took her face in his hands and kissed her. His warm tears hit her cheeks. Icy droplets fell from Emily's own eyes. She wanted to sit there in a passionate embrace for the three hours until sunrise in the Dark region so there would no longer be a reason to have to leave. Instead, she withdrew her face and whispered, "We can't let her die."

Will moved his hand from behind Emily's head, bringing with it the blonde hair tangled between fingers. He held the tips of her hair out into the rising sunlight and Emily could see a slight golden glow come off of them. He let the hair slide out from his fingertips, then looked Emily in the eye, "Off to kill Wit, I suppose?"

Emily stood, designing each motion so she would face away from the sun. She reached under her cloak to feel in her bag—the blade was still there and the vial still intact. She had wrapped a piece of cloth around the glass to protect it. Thankfully, it had done enough to cushion the fragile flask from the jolts and bounces while sprinting down and over the foothills, "Do you have enough energy for this?"

Will stood, brushing the dirt from the ground off of his pants and shoes. He was not using magic to make himself more presentable, so it was obvious he didn't have extra energy to spare, but he said the portal incantation and it opened before them, "Enough energy to send one through to Wit's residence."

Emily didn't want to ask for more than what Will could do, but also didn't want to go through alone. What if Wit had others with him? What if he somehow knew she was coming?

"Bring yourself through as soon as you can?" Emily pleaded.

"As soon as I can," Will repeated, kissing Emily's hand.

Just before she stepped in, she turned to Will, "But when this is over, we need to talk about whatever this," she gestured quickly between the two of them, "is." She huffed as she decided to go in for one more kiss. Kissing him felt too nice and it seemed wrong to not take every opportunity to enjoy it while she was here.

She stepped through the dark circle only to have it close immediately after she exited the other side. The darkness did not leave and her eyes quickly adjusted to the night outside of a tall building. Solid walls of grey stone reached toward the sky. Emily could find no windows except some small arrow slits on the turrets on the corners. The air was humid and the stone dripped with condensation.

Emily looked away from the castle, only to find she was standing near the edge of a cliff with nothingness in each direction. Lights twinkled in the far distance; this was the home of someone who clearly wanted personal space.

A black metal door stood alone, the only decoration on this wall of the castle. She knocked and the sound echoed loudly inside. Although she felt no chill, she did feel goosebumps tickle her skin. Strange how she would still be uneasy when she herself was now something that went bump in the night. There was no answer at the door, but Emily did not know what else to do. She waited until she heard echoing footsteps from inside the building and knocked again.

The door opened a crack. One eye could be seen well above Emily's head, illuminated by the moonlight, while no light escaped from inside.

"I wish to speak with Wit," Emily commanded.

"The master of the house is not in," The voice was so deep it caused vibrations in Emily's core, like a growl of an immense beast.

"Tell his driver to retrieve him," Emily demanded. "Daughter of Champion requests his presence immediately." She began to push her way inside.

The demon who answered the door backed off, but did not take his eyes off Emily, studying her to settle his disbelief. His body was incredibly muscular and his head like that of a bull. When Emily removed the hood of her cloak, the minotaur bowed awkwardly, finding balance on his cloven feet, "Your Highness, I did not recognize you," he raised himself, but did not make eye contact with Emily again, "Please wait wherever you wish—I will call for his driver."

Emily took in the great room, which from the looks of it was as tall as the building itself. It was nearly completely empty and almost completely dark. A faint glow of light could be seen coming from another room through an open door, but no other lights were there. Emily's eyes adjusted just fine, but she understood why the servant had taken so long to recognize her face. The emptiness made the room look intimidatingly large; for having lived so long, he had not accumulated much stuff.

A large fireplace was the focal point of one wall with an overmantle that stretched all the way to the ceiling. Emily admired the intricate patterns that circled around a central carved face—a lovely woman whose disgusted eyes seemed to pierce Emily's soul. Why would this be his only decoration?

Emily stared at the woman and the image stared back. The longer she looked into those stone eyes, the more uncomfortable Emily was in her own skin. She forced herself to look away, down at the fireplace below. She put her hand on the coals and willed them to ignite. She could feel warmth in her hands, but nothing close to what she would need to get the fire going. She fiddled with her fingers until she could feel her fingertips buzz, then touched the coals once more. An electric arc shot from her fingertips to the fuel and started a low smoulder, which quickly ignited into a full-fledged fire. Emily sat on the ground before the fireplace, watching the flames dance.

It was only moments later that she heard the metal door close. She looked back, expecting to see the bull demon, but jumped in her skin when she saw Wit taking off his cloak.

"Still attempting to warm yourself by a fire?" Wit laughed, "You will realize soon enough that it is a fool's errand. The chill will never leave."

"How did you...?" Emily began before she was interrupted.

"I was waiting outside the palace," Wit walked quickly to her. "I wanted to be sure you were alright. I ran home as soon as my driver told me you were here." He grazed his hands over her face, her arms, "How are you feeling? You recovered quite quickly. I was unable to even move for a week when I changed," He lifted her face to meet his eyes, "But you were not just a human, no. You were much stronger. I should have known you would complete the transformation easily."

Emily could hear past his feigned concern. "You tried to kill my sister." Her words were sharp.

Wit bent down to kiss Emily on the neck on top of her scar, "Your Highness, I *have* killed your sister."

Chapter Nineteen

I just need to stab him now. Just one, two, and done. Emily imagined the feeling of the blade sinking into his flesh. Could she bring herself to kill someone? Her hand felt for her bag under her cloak, but rested there while she sought more information, "Why did you want to kill her?"

"You have not been a vampire long," Wit noted in a condescending manner, "But once you are around for a few hundred years, you realize the only ones who serve your own interest are your own kind. We do not want a demon reigning over the region. We certainly do not want a human as our queen. If your father had no heir, there would be another Grand Trial upon his death, and the victor may be more," he paused for dramatic effect, "sympathetic to our plight."

"But then I showed up," Emily fueled the continuation of the story.

"Will brought you," he sneered, matching the look of revulsion on the sculpture's face, "Not only a human, but someone who knows nothing of our world. I should have killed you that first day, but Will would have pieced together that I was behind your sister's sickness—he is not a complete dunce. Disgusting how you fell over yourself to be close to me. A game

I miss from the human world, luring young maidens, but you were too easy. There was no hunt, just a pathetic girl desperate for affection."

Emily was speechless. Her hand worked its way into the satchel. She gripped the bejeweled hilt and seethed through gritted teeth, "You have not killed her yet."

Wit withdrew a pocket watch from his vest, "Less than an hour and she will be, essentially, dead."

Emily lowered her head and arched her back, a panther readying itself to pounce, "Not if I kill you first." She flexed her fingers on the dagger, the metal pressed into her palm.

Wit stretched out his arms, indicating the emptiness around them, "How?" His voice echoed in the far corners and bounced off the ceiling, "I am an immortal being."

In one swift motion, the dagger was out of the bag and the tip was pressed against Wit's chest. He held his hands up, his face full of amusement.

Emily pushed the tip slightly deeper into his vest, "You may be immortal, but you are not invincible." Emily willed her hand to press the blade into his chest, but it would not move. She had more that she wanted to know, "Why did you make me into one of you?"

"That was a mistake," Wit sounded apologetic, but then his tone changed to mockery, "I meant to kill you." His hand swept through the air between them and came out the other side with the dagger in his grasp. He clutched it by the blade, but threw it in the air and caught it again by the hilt.

Emily tried to back away, but Wit grabbed her by her right arm. She could feel his fingers dig deep into the soft tissue. When he pulled her in to kiss her violently, she slapped his face with her free left hand.

"You do not deserve the gift I have given you," he brought his face close to hers once again, "You ungrateful wench." His right arm swung forward, thrusting the blade up under Emily's ribs.

The blade was hot. He let go of her arm, letting her collapse to the ground. Emily reached to her side, expecting to feel blood oozing out from a wound. Instead, she found the dagger lodged in her side, already scabbed into place. Every move she made caused it to cut deeper, opening the wound momentarily until it closed itself again. She made a half-effort of removing the blade, but it was stuck. It would cause a great deal of pain to move it, she realized. Sitting as still as she could, Emily accepted that she would only have one shot. She needed to make it count.

"What did you expect?" Wit walked away from the fireplace and Emily slumped before it, "I cannot die. You cannot die. We can entertain ourselves for eons battling each other, but in the end we will both still be here to sicken the other."

"You asked me to stay with you," Emily whimpered, intentionally sounding pathetic, "You said I was stronger than my sister. You said…" She made her best attempt at tears and, given the sadistic expression on Wit's face, he fell for it.

He glided to her, but did not make eye contact. He stared into the fireplace, letting the orange glow bounce off his face, "I lied." He stood there a moment longer before bending down to put himself in Emily's line of sight, "And you were foolish enough to believe me. I would have kept you here, letting you think you belong, then once I confirmed your sister was dead, I would kill you." He put his hand on Emily's right shoulder.

Emily grabbed the hilt with her left hand. She felt a snap in her side as she pulled the hilt but left the blade. They both looked down to see a thin, pointed stick that had been concealed within the metal. As Wit turned to try to back away, Emily drove the stake into his chest. The resistance was not like a blade into flesh, instead his chest began to crumble like broken rocks around the wood. The effect spread from that point, slowly encompassing his entire body. Before it reached his face, he turned his head back towards the fireplace, gazing at the image of the woman. A hopeful smile graced his lips as he spoke one last word, "Margaret."

Emily was left with rubble on her lap and on the ground before her while small pieces of debris carried on the hot air coming off the fireplace. She looked up to see the minotaur, standing just inside the open door. His eyes narrowed as he lowered his head.

Emily reached for the blade in her side. She would need something more than a stick to take on this beast of a creature. She picked at the bit of metal protruding from her rib but could not grasp it well enough to pull. The bull stormed toward her, snarling. He moved slowly, but purposefully, retaliation in his eyes.

As he raised two clenched fists above his head, poised to slam down on Emily, she raised her hands to defend herself. She waited for the imminent pain, but a sudden *thunk* was heard above her head. Emily looked up to see the demon stunned and collapsing off to the side. The space he vacated revealed a small, purple demoness with a long metal rod in her hands. She rushed over to the collapsed minotaur and lightly touched the blood seeping from his head, "Ooh," she shrank back, "I might have swung a bit too hard."

"How did you...?" Emily started, but Daughter of Brawn was too skilled a chatterer to make her friend guide the conversation.

"Empath had me follow Wit," she recounted with a nonchalant voice, the whole time eyeing the unconscious body beside them uncomfortably, "He was again outside the palace all night, but did not wait until sunup to leave as he normally had. His driver had some words with him and he sprinted on foot in this direction. His driver was to follow with the coach, so I hid inside. Of course we were not as quick as a vampire, but we made much better time than if I had tried to walk the entire way.

We pulled up in front of this," she looked up at the ceiling, "cozy place," she paused, taking in the enormity of the room, then proceeded with her usual chipper manner, "Before the driver noticed I was there, I managed to take his cane," she clasped the metal bar and used it to point toward the door, "rendered him insensible. Concealed myself once more when I heard the minotaur approach, but he became enraged upon seeing the driver. Entered in time to see him make his way toward you, snuck up behind him, and here we are." She ended with a proud smile.

Emily laughed in disbelief. Each chuckle came with a sharp pain from the metal still embedded in her side. She realized she still held the wooden dagger in her hand and handed it to Daughter of Brawn, "Killed Wit."

Daughter of Brawn admired the weapon, then looked around for a body. Emily simply gazed down at the pile of rocky rubble strewn about the floor between them. Daughter of Brawn fell back from her knees to her rear and scurried backward on hands and heels. When she collected herself, she asked, "Because he bit you?"

"Nah," Emily reached again to pick at the thorn in her side, "The only way to undo the effects of the potion was to kill him, but I can't say it didn't feel good." She cocked her head, "Do you happen to know of a Margaret?"

"No, your Highness," Daughter of Brawn was toying with the wooden blade, poking it into her fingertip while spinning the hilt, "Does this mean we will have *two* princesses?"

Emily brought out the flask, "Unfortunately, no," she swirled the pink liquid around and it rose against the sides of the spherical container, "This little vampire is turning human. Completely human."

Daughter of Brawn slammed the jeweled wooden blade onto the stone floor, making a loud *clink*. She slid it to Emily, "You should keep that in your possession. In the wrong hands you would suffer the same fate as…" she trailed off as her eyes rested on the remains of Wit.

Emily wondered if her friend had even understood what she had just told her, as her response seemed to have glossed over the subject. She placed the vial back into its protective cloth in her bag and picked up the wooden-stick-on-a-gaudy-hilt. She looked closely to see that at the base of where the blade had been were small clamps in an open position. Curious, she took the wooden piece and aligned it with the hole in the blade, sliding it back into place. Another *snap*. She tugged on it once more to find it securely in one piece. She let out a deep breath through pursed lips and yanked. The blade ripped free from her scabbed flesh. Emily yelped in pain. The dagger slipped through her trembling fingers and she clutched her side with both hands, again expecting blood but feeling nothing but a crusty scab.

They both laid on the ground, staring up at the ceiling that seemed miles away. Daughter of Brawn, not one to let silence linger, asked, "Where is his Lordship?"

"Will? He had to rest after creating so many portals," Emily wiggled so her back would lie flat against the ground, stretching her tight muscles, "He should be here soon, I would think. Has the sun risen yet?"

Daughter of Brawn made a noise of affirmation, "It should be rising now. I do not wish to leave you trapped here alone, but I should tell Empath and your father what has happened." She rose to her feet and picked up the metal cane. She began twirling it in her hand, "I think I am going to keep this." She used it to poke the unconscious body lying on the ground, "He should remain in this state for some time, but you will be able to handle him easily if he does awaken," she smiled at Emily, "So long as you keep any blades from your ribs."

Emily reached for the dagger and secured it into its sheath, then put it into her bag, nodding at Daughter of Brawn as she left through the front door. The room seemed even larger now that she was alone once again. She stared at the bull-headed figure. *Well, mostly alone.*

She brought herself next to the fire—the chill never did leave, but the warmth on her skin still felt nice. Sitting there for some time, she reflected on the past week. She remembered the anxious, foolish girl who had arrived in this world. When she was human once more, could she return to being the same person she once was? Could she ever be happy in the human world? Perhaps this new confidence would carry with her, even if the power that spurred that confidence would be gone forever. How much was it going to hurt knowing her sister and father were alive and she could never see them again? The questions swirled in her mind as she watched the tips of the fire leap and bend.

She could not tell how long had passed when a burst of bright light came through the door, the screech of the hinges breaking Emily's trance.

A relieved Will closed the door and rushed over to where she sat, "Is it done? Did you save her?"

Emily smiled weakly and nodded. She had just succeeded in saving her sister's life; why did she feel disappointed? She could go home. She got to be a normal human being with normal human problems. Where was the excitement in that, though?

"Oh?" Will's enthusiasm quickly turned to dissatisfaction as well, "Oh." Perhaps he had more reason to be upset than Emily did—he lost his friend while Emily was only losing people and power she had known for less than a fortnight. Will noticed the body on the floor, "Am I to assume this and the driver were your handiwork?"

Emily arched her eyebrows, "Actually, Daughter of Brawn. She took real quickly to knocking guys out. We need to keep an eye on them, though. Not sure how long they'll stay under."

Will wrapped his arm around Emily as they leaned back in front of the fire. He asked no more questions, and Emily preferred it that way. She curled in close to Will and laid her head on his chest, listening to his heartbeat. She sat still, searching within herself for her own heart's beat, but could not feel it. Eventually, Will laid down completely on the stone floor, too tired to remain upright. Emily laid down with him, tucked under his arm with her head over his heart, but did not sleep the entire day. She was haunted by the image of Wit's crumbling face each time she closed her eyes, but she gave herself the excuse that she would need to remain alert in case one of the two incapacitated staff came to.

Chapter Twenty

Will woke up around midday. Emily hadn't moved—there was no need to. She wanted to stay there with him forever, though the ambiance could be improved upon. He pulled a watch from his vest pocket, "The sun is setting where your sister is," he said with sleep in his voice as he rubbed Emily's arm, "are you ready to go meet her?"

There was no use delaying the inevitable. Emily untucked herself from under Will's arm and rose to her feet, "Let's go." She secured her bag, checking to be sure the glass was still intact. She felt a twinge of disappointment when she found it was.

Before he got up, Will pulled rocks from his pocket and crawled across the floor, placing them in specific positions. He went back to adjust them multiple times, making sure they were just so. There was no pattern to them that Emily could see—a group of three rocks, a large space, two stones, another space, then five in a row with a small space before a single rock. The only reason to it was that they all ended up in a circle about six feet wide.

"Are you sure you have the energy for this? You haven't rested long."

"It is a different kind of magic," Will said as he put the last stone in the exact position he needed, "I will be pulling energy from the world, not from myself." He brought himself alongside Emily, both of them staring down at the patterned circle of rocks, "We could have left the moment I got here had the sun in the human world not killed you the moment we got there." He turned to face Emily, "We will have one half of an hour before I have to return with your sister."

Emily continued to look at the floor, "Got it." She knew this was when she was supposed to say goodbye, but she didn't want to. She was terrible at goodbyes—hence why she did not suggest to Will that she return to the palace to see Empath, Daughter of Brawn, or her father one last time. She would rather just move on as quickly as possible.

Will said an incantation that was different from the one he used to take them to and from the Mountains. This one was darker, with a harsher accent to the words. The portal looked the same, but it felt different. A wind was pulling them towards it. Will shouted over the noise of the gust, "It is going to leave you a little disoriented. Do not try to rise too quickly as you did the last time."

They stepped through together. It was not instantaneous. Emily remembered the feeling—it was as if her mind was being squeezed while her body stretched like elastic in incomprehensible ways. She heard screams through the blackness—were they hers? Why did they sound so far away? She could see nothing but black.

She opened her eyes to see a dark sky with a streetlight illuminating the rain that was falling down onto her face. It was solid concrete under her back, all of it wet, but the tips of her hair were being pulled away from her. She turned to see she was at the edge of the sidewalk and her hair was hanging off the edge into the street where the rainfall was collecting and running downhill. She wasn't tired or sick from the portal—she felt completely fine. She was able to stand up easily, but she did so slowly just to be sure. She got to her feet and heard Will's voice from the ground behind her to her right.

"Home sweet home?"

Emily turned her face toward him, but her expression was lost. She stared, slack-jawed in his direction. The rain was falling hard—harder than normal for this area. It felt warm on Emily's skin as it streaked down her face.

This place wasn't home. It was where she slept. Home was the bookstore. Home was where she felt comfortable. Home was where she had people she cared for.

Will saw her face, "I'm sorry. Your dad says that frequently. I thought it was a human phrase."

"It is," Emily turned back toward the apartment building in front of them. It was her residence. Her sister was still in there, hopefully awake and wondering what was going on. No lights were on in her window, but she could have simply not known how light switches worked.

Will took his time getting up. He rubbed his hands over his outfit—his expression was momentarily confused before he realized he could not dry his clothes with magic and gave up. He stepped right beside Emily, their arms dangling in a way their hands were a hair's width from touching. "We did make it to the correct location, though?"

"Yep," Emily paused to take a long breath, "the corner of Grey Street and the end of the world." She began the walk toward the steps that would lead to her door. The cool air carried the smell of evergreen trees. It burned the inside of her nose like the sharp cold of winter air. She felt for the bag on her right hip, checking once again for the glass container—soon she could drink it and this whole thing would be over. Just what she wanted, right?

Will led the way. He held Emily's hand as they went up the stairs—she couldn't balance herself on the wooden handrail without suffering excruciating pain. The front door was closed, but unlocked. He pushed it open and Emily heard the familiar squeak when the door was open about six inches. She had always meant to ask to have that fixed. Emily's shoulder brushed the door frame as she walked in and she could feel heat from the wood penetrate her sleeve.

The moment he entered the room, Will stopped in his tracks, staring at the bed at the other end of the studio apartment. He raised his hand to his gaping mouth. Emily turned the corner to find her sister still lying in the bed. She rushed over and kneeled on the carpet beside the bed. She brushed her sister's hair out of her face to find the veins in her face had turned black, while her lips were purple and her eyes sunken. She turned back to Will, "She was supposed to be better! What happened?" Her voice lost its composure.

"It was not him," Will said as he stared into the corner of the room, "It must have been someone else."

"No," Emily said brusquely, "Daeron described him to a T and Wit admitted that he gave her the potion. He was the one who ordered the potion," Emily put her hands over her mouth as she remembered Daeron's query, "But I asked the wrong question. He ordered it," she paused, eyes wide, willing herself to reveal the truth, "but it wasn't his blood." Emily turned back to her sister. She felt her skin—still warm. She was still alive, but barely. There was not enough time to go back and do this all again. Something had to be done right now—something drastic.

Will stood behind Emily, finally getting a closer look at his fiancée. His face contorted as tears began to well up in his eyes. Emily stood to face him and turned his face to make eye contact.

"Do you trust me?" She held both of his hands in hers, interlacing their fingers.

He cleared his throat and took in a deep breath, "I trust you."

Emily pulled their hands down behind her, pulling him closer. She kissed him and they lingered there for a few moments. Emily ended the kiss by pushing him away forcefully, causing him to stumble to the floor.

In an instant, Emily was leaning over her sister, the cotton of the bedsheets irritating her palms. She sank her teeth into the space where her sister's neck met her shoulder. The first gush of blood made her nauseous, but she bit down harder to override her gag reflex. Once the taste hit her tongue, it was the most pleasant sensation she had ever experienced. The salty and metallic taste coated her taste buds. The warmth as she swallowed finally heated that part of her that had been ice. She wanted to keep drinking, to fill herself with this warmth as long as she could.

Will screamed from the floor, where he had barely had time to pull himself up, "Emily! What are you doing?"

Emily snapped back to reality. She had to stop. She didn't want to, but she had to. She took one more long draw as she reached into the pouch and pulled out the vial. As she pulled herself away, she uncorked it and placed the opening into her sister's mouth. The small stopper scalded her hand as she tilted the vial and watched the liquid slowly drain.

A forceful hand pulled her away, throwing her to the ground. Will finally saw what had been done and quickly removed the vial from Daughter of Champion's lips. He held it up, almost completely empty, then looked at Emily, whispering, "What have you done?"

Emily sat up and wiped the blood from her lips and chin, "I hope I just saved my sister's life. The Vengeful Sleep potion only works on humans, not on vampires. She was a vampire for a moment. I just hope it was long enough."

Will looked back at Daughter of Champion, whose skin began to spring back to life. The black veins retreated; her lips lost their purple hue. She began to breathe deep breaths, her chest rising and falling. Will brought the remaining drops of liquid to Emily, who sat on the floor, unsure of what to do next. He held the potion out to her.

Emily took the round flask and caressed it with her fingers, "But I've already drank someone else's blood. It won't work."

"Please," Will pleaded. "Just try."

Emily lightly pushed him aside and went past him to sit at the foot of her bed, "We need to make sure she is alright first." They waited in silence. Emily alternated her gaze between her sister to the drops of pink liquid in their clear container. As minutes passed, her sister began to develop a rosy hue and move in her sleep, turning to her side and letting out a light moan as she settled into a restful sleep.

"I do believe your strategy has worked," Will gestured to the vial in Emily's hand. "Now it is your turn."

"No," Emily looked at Will and looked into his eyes. "I'm going back. One sister here, one sister there." She held the flask out to Will, "This is for you, if you want to stay here with her."

Will looked at the vial in Emily's hand for a moment before bending down to retrieve the cork Emily had dropped on the ground. He sealed it once more and pushed Emily's hand away, "Your sister is my good friend and I have made sure she is safe. Now I need to be there to support the future queen."

Emily grasped the vial in one hand, placed her other hand on her chest, and let out her breath, "Oh, thank goodness, I wasn't sure what way that was going to go." She stood and held him in her arms, kissing him once more before she asked, "How long do we have before the portal opens?"

Will looked at the clock on the wall, "About ten minutes. Why do you ask?"

Emily looked down at her sister, still sleeping in the bed, "I'm not sure how long it will be until she is awake. There is some stuff she will need to know."

While Will sat on the edge of the bed, waiting for further signs of life from Daughter of Champion, Emily rushed around her small apartment, gathering things. She plugged in her dead phone and sent off a short message. She got her wallet and took out her ID card. She found her birth certificate and yelled profanities as the paper burned her skin while she carried it to the coffee table, setting it beside a photo album. She found a pad of paper but went to the bathroom to get a pair of nitrile gloves to wear as she wrote.

> *Daughter of Champion,*
>
> *My name is Emily. I am your sister. You were poisoned by someone in your world. We failed in reversing it, but we did find a way to save your life. You were a vampire for all of a few seconds, but you are now human. As I am now no longer human, I must take your place there and you must take my place here.*
>
> *I'm sorry to have to tell you that our mom died three years ago. She was just as lovely as the painting over the dining room door and she would have loved to hear you tell her stories of your world.*
>
> *I've left legal documents; you can use them to prove you are me. I asked Abigail to come over—she was mom's friend from the bookstore and might actually believe this story. I also left a book of images of me and mom so you can get to know her a little.*
>
> *I promise to try my best to take care of the kingdom. I promise to take care of our dad and Will.*
>
> *Have a great life here,*
> *Emily*

Emily removed one picture of her and her mom from the album—the last one taken before her mother became seriously ill—and placed it into her bag. She went to the kitchen and hand-washed the dishes in the sink for the last time, still wearing the gloves because she wasn't about to grab the cotton dish rag with her bare hands. She dried all the dishes and put them away neatly. Then she removed and threw out the gloves.

Emily went to put her hand on Will's shoulder, "It's almost time. Should we go?"

Will nodded, giving Daughter of Champion's hand one last squeeze before he once again led Emily through the maze of wooden furniture, doors, and rails. They made it back to the edge of the sidewalk and waited less than a minute before the dark circle opened for them. Emily took a deep breath, readying herself for the journey. She stepped through, hand in hand with Will, never looking back.

Epilogue

At a wide table sat seven individuals with gaunt features. The two elves' appearance were due to their overall stature, the demon's due to age, while for the vampires it was just their natural, sunken appearance.

"Will the subject please step forward," an old elf with long, white hair said as he looked over a piece of parchment in front of him. He held it up to see better.

A woman stepped into the middle of the circular stone floor. None of the seven bothered to look at her. They all kept their eyes on papers on their desks or on the speaking tribunal member.

The elf continued with his frail voice, "The tribunal has met to discuss your trial. We believe it is a valid trial and will grant your request to be named." He put down the parchment and finally looked at the woman. Her blonde hair was down, falling over her shoulders. She wore a red dress that hugged her body and rested on her natural hips. She had no markings or indications she had ever been a demoness. She had a black scar, however, on her shoulder where she had been bitten.

A vampire, the newest member of the tribunal, was the next to speak. "We find that the subject has committed many atrocities against the rightful heir, against the kingdom, and against a fellow vampire. Because of this, some on the tribunal refuse to give a favorable name."

From the far left of the table came the next voice, the demon, "Yet these acts were in defense of her own life and that of her sister," he seemed to be speaking directly to the vampire who had spoken before him, "So some shall not give an unfavorable name."

The vampire glared at the demon, unhappy with that decision, but the demon continued, "We have each chosen a name for you and, since we could not come to an agreement, have decided to let you choose the tribunal member who will name you."

The woman eyed each of the members, all of whom were finally looking down at her. She felt each of their stares. The vampires gave a look of spite, while the elves and demon were more neutral. Would she wear a distasteful name as a badge of honor, or hope a fellow demon would provide something more palatable? Perhaps the elves would have creative names that would suit her. She turned to the hallway behind her where her fiancé waited. The arched doorway was aglow with firelight, but she could see the outline of his shadow nodding encouragingly. She turned back toward the tribunal.

"Honored judges," The woman curtsied slowly in a dramatic gesture, remaining bowed as she continued, "In learning about the history of our region, I have learned about each of you and am honored to get to choose one of you to give me a name. I trust each of you has chosen a name I could take with pride, knowing it suits me based on the actions of my natural trial. Based on his incredible reputation both during his time on the tribunal as well as before he was called to this assignment, I would like to ask Judge Prophecy to choose my name."

The dark-skinned elf who had yet to speak sat straighter. His white hair was pulled back in small braids and his white eyes shone down on the woman as he looked at her. He was not surprised she had called on him; his intuition told him that she might and that she would appreciate the name he gave her. "Daughter of Champion," he began in a booming voice.

"Second Daughter of Champion," the vampire who had spoken before scoffed.

"*Second* Daughter of Champion," the white-eyed elf continued, "Based on your actions of concealing yourself and wearing the identity of your sister, impersonating her for a considerable amount of time, and now taking on her role as your own, I decree that you shall henceforth be known as Mask."

All seven men at the table repeated the name in unison, "Mask."

The elf then stood, the sound of metal screeching on stone echoing through the large room, "Mask, being the first named child of Champion, you are now to be recognized as the rightful heir to the throne of the Dark Region."

Meanwhile, in the human world, two women were sitting across from each other drinking coffee. The young brunette was recounting fantastic stories of another world while the older woman listened intently. While most would not have believed the extraordinary tales, this woman understood that it was the truth, as she happened to know a great deal about the magical creatures that still remained in the human world.

About the Author

Andrea Fink lives north of Seattle, Washington with her husband and daughter. Throughout her years of teaching elementary school, she has encouraged her students to follow their dreams. Now, she is tackling her own, finally writing the series she has been sitting on for a decade. In addition to wanting to write a book, she has also dreamed of completing a transatlantic crossing, becoming a confectioner, being an extra in a movie, living abroad, and voicing a cartoon character.

Facebook: Andrea Fink, Author
Instagram: @andrea.as.an.author

Made in the USA
Monee, IL
16 February 2022

90699416R00132